BIRDWATCHING
AT THE
END OF THE WORLD

BIRDWATCHING
AT THE
END OF THE WORLD

G.W. DEXTER

NewCon Press
England

First edition, published in the UK August 2024
by NewCon Press
41 Wheatsheaf Road, Alconbury Weston, Cambs, PE28 4LF, UK

NCP335 (hardback)
NCP336 (softback)

10 9 8 7 6 5 4 3 2 1

ISBN: 978-1-914953-84-2 (hardback)
978-1-914953-85-9 (softback)

Cover Art by Ben Baldwin
Map and seagulls by G.W. Dexter
Editing and typesetting by Ian Whates
Cover layout by Ian Whates

For Mimi

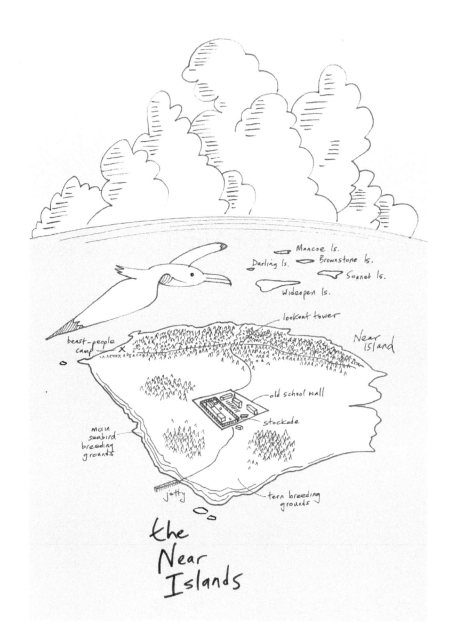

Mancoe Is.

Darling Is.   Brownstone Is.

Soanet Is.

Wideopen Is.

lookout tower

Near Island

beast-people camp

X

old school wall

stockade

main seabird breeding grounds

jetty

tern breeding grounds

the
Near
Islands

ONE

I am Stephen Ballantyne. Before the end of the world, I was a pupil at Near School for Girls, Near Island, Aberdeen AB12 3LE.

But hold hard, I hear you say: Stephen is not a girls' name.

Correct. I was the headmistress's son, and in accordance with tradition and convenience, I boarded at – and attended lessons at – the school where she – my mother – presided. And felt none the worse for it.

The school was the only building on Near, the largest island in the otherwise uninhabited Near Islands. These constitute a nature reserve, and lie in the choppy waters of the North Sea, about thirteen miles distant from Aberdeen.

Near is not a large island: perhaps a hundred and twenty acres, with a roundish shape. It is also, unusually for islands of these latitudes, forested, particularly in the eastern half, below the central ridge. The trees, all Scots pines, were planted around the time of the school's founding in 1903.

The girls were boarders, of course. Mainly of British yeoman stock. A couple from foreign parts: Fritzi Pietsch, from Hamm, for example. Or Fritzi Hamm, from Pietsch; I could never remember. And even more exotically, Camilla Moon Khan, from Mymensingh, her very name conjuring up the milky mystery of midnight mosques.

My own father, you might be interested to hear, was from Spain. Yes, I am the issue of a lily-white headmistress and a swarthy Spanish gentleman. By profession he was a museologist, visiting London for a conference. It was there that they met. My mother had an interest in Spanish antiques.

Although he was not so very old.

So I, Stephen Ballantyne, am Anglo-Spanish. Nevertheless, I have lived all my life – as far back as I can remember – on Near. I have had no contact with any subcontinental relative. My Anglo-Spanishness, or Ibero-Anglianity, is somewhat notional. Until someone brings it up.

My mother and I formed an odd partnership. She, head of the school, I, head of the household. Physically too we were an odd couple: she, storky, pasty, angular, and I, compact, brown, rodentine. She, well-beloved by the students, I, tolerated by those same students.

As in any close couple, we sought one another's opinions on questions of moment. What about the VHV block? Does it need refurbishment? What's your opinion, Stephen? Are the Bunsen burner hoses looking worn? And the vegetable garden. Is it worth the effort? What would you do?

I felt these sessions were important. She was a woman of many dilemmas. Dilemmas, one might say, were the one thing she was permanently on the horns of.

Let us suppose a sticky-handed girl (seriously-poised pencil, braces, mouldering half-eaten sandwich in recesses of school bag) is taking a survey of her classmates in 1975 – early 1975 – and has alighted on me, her coeval. A boy, of the school and yet not of the school.

'What's your favourite animal?'

'Crocodile.'

Effortful writing. Anne Heaviside, gangling, dim.

'What's your favourite food?'

'Evaporated milk.'

'That's not a food.'

'It depends on how much you evaporate it.'

'It has to be a food.'

'All right.' I encogitate. 'Soup.'

'Soup isn't a food either.'

'Of course it is,' I say, seriously surprised. 'You could survive on soup.'

'Miss, is soup a food?'

Miss Roughan, on break duty: Miss Roughan will be annihilated somewhere in France in about a month's time.

'It is a sort of food, yes,' she says absently. 'It's a liquid food.'

'Do I have to put it down?' Anne asks her, eyeing me. She wants me to see her being forced.

'If that is Stephen's favourite food,' says Miss Roughan, with a kind smile, 'then put it down, although he is a growing boy and I would have thought he'd prefer something a little more substantial.'

'Soup,' I pronounce.

'All right,' Anne says. She enters the information. 'What's your favourite colour?'

'Blue.'

'Do you have a pet at home, and if so, what's his name?'

But all the school knows about my pet, so she doesn't even wait for my reply. 'Albert,' she says, writing.

Albert is about six inches long. He has greyish overparts and buff netherparts. He eats mainly snails. He is a rock pipit. I found him when I was thirteen years old, and he himself only a teenager in rock-pipit years. He had broken his leg. He lives in my room, or on my shoulder. He is not allowed in any enclosed area except my room and the halls.

Actually, I don't know what sex Albert is. Male and female rock pipits look identical.

But none of this matters a great deal. Anne Heaviside can be dispensed with an as interlocutor, even though we have not yet got onto my favourite drink (lemonade shandy), favourite book (*The Inimitable Jeeves*), favourite TV Show (*The Fall and Rise of Reginald Perrin*) and favourite pop group (Queen). This story isn't really about me. I am, as a person, not very interesting, not very remarkable, full of faults of all kinds. My chief fault, I suppose, is my reckless tendency toward self-effacement.

Though who am I to say what my chief fault is? Some may say that my chief fault is that my knees are ill-formed. I'm looking at them now. They are mismatched.

If I efface myself, it is only so another may surface.

My first memory of Pearl Wyss dates to about seven years ago. She had just joined the school.

Our class had made a trip to a farm on the mainland, and we were seated in a species of barn or byre. Let us call it an outbuilding. There were thirty of us, some now deceased – Barbara Pulmow, Caroline Kett, Yolanda Vane-Hovell-Vane – and some yet undeceased – Kay Hawkins, Polly Findhorn, Beulah Gaze. We were all twelve years old.

The farmer stood before us with his cow. He was an ugly fellow. He looked like he would smell quite foul if you got too close to him; and not a smell of farms but a smell of what he wanted from you if he could get it.

'Right, why do we use artificial insemination to get a cow pregnant? You,' he said, pointing to Barbara Pulmow, now deceased.

'Is it because it's better for them?' Barbara ventured.

'No, not really,' the man said, affecting puzzlement at Barbara's stupidity. 'It's better for us. We don't want to keep a lot of bulls around, because they take feeding and looking after.'

He gave the cow's rump a pat. A fat black and white cow. It munched.

'All right, now. I'm going to tell you how we do it. Listen carefully.'

This man was quite at his ease in front of an outbuilding full of girls (and your narrator). He exuded malevolence, which was probably what helped him along in life in general.

'Number one,' he began. 'You've got to get the cow at the right time. There's an eighteen-hour window in every cycle. We know she's in the right window because she's discharging out of her rear end.' He pointed. 'Or she might be calling to other cows. Or she might be letting other cows mount her.'

He smiled. No-one answered this smile, because it was the smile of a man who knew that all the girls present were thinking of themselves as females.

'All right,' he continued. 'When you know she's ready for it, you've got to get her so she's relaxed, and so it's got to be an area like this where she's happy and there's lots of food. Then you get out your straw. That's what's got the semen in it.'

He held up a straw. It was essentially like a drinking straw, though longer. Being full of semen, it had little of the functionality of a drinking straw.

'You've got your sexed semen and your mixed semen. Whatever you've got, take it out of the cooler and put it in warm water for the right amount of time. Twenty seconds for a small one and forty seconds for a big one. The straw, that is, not the cow. Then take your gun.'

He held up his gun. It was a thing like an ogre's hypodermic needle, about two feet long, with a blue plastic butt and trigger.

'Take the straw, put it in the gun and cut the end off. I'm not going to do it now. Clean the cow up a bit and put on your glove and lubricant. Then put your arm up the cow's arse.'

The man lifted up the cow's tail and indicated the area. Not needing to look at the arse, being long familiar with it, he looked at us instead.

'You're thinking why the arse?' he said. 'Because you use your fingers to find the cervix through the arse. Then, when you've got it, you put in the gun.'

Perhaps you, dear reader, are expecting that there would be groans or giggles from the schoolgirl spectators at this point? No. They were not playful or giggly. They were petrified.

'Use your elbow on your gun hand to pull the skin down so the lips spread out,' said the farmer. He mimed the procedure. 'Then take the gun and guide it in so it finds the cervix. I'm not going to do it now because this one isn't ready for it. You pass it through the canal into the uterus. Then you press the trigger and count to five like you're counting off seconds. 5,4,3,2,1. Lift-off. Pull the gun out. Never serve a cow if she's already pregnant. You'll lose the calf.'

He stood back from the animal, letting the gun dangle at his side. Then he swivelled and jabbed a forefinger at Pearl Wyss.

'Right, you. Come up here,' he said.

Pearl was at the front. She was one of the smallest and mousiest-looking of all the girls.

She walked forward and went to stand next to the cow. She was just about the same height as the cow's rear. She looked like a little old lady. She had shadows under her eyes and a long, puffy upper lip.

'Now what did I just say?' the man demanded.

It was deeply shocking. There was me thinking that the worst thing that could possibly happen in this vile place would be listening to this farmer-man describe a procedure of maximal sordidness and disrespect for cow-kind. But no. It seemed he wanted a bit of fun too.

I wondered if he did this when the audience were all boys. I concluded he probably did.

Pearl lifted her head and stared into the middle distance, looking neither at the cow, nor the man, nor her audience. We were all thanking our lucky stars it wasn't us.

'It's important to do the artificial insemination at the right time,' Pearl said. 'There's an eighteen-hour window in every cycle. There are certain signs that tell you whether she's ready: discharge, allowing other cows to mount her, or calling to other cows. The cow's got to be relaxed, so it's got to be done in an area where she's happy and there's lots of food. After you've removed the semen straw – mixed or sexed – you put it in warm water for the right amount of time. Twenty seconds for a small one and forty seconds for a big one. Wipe it dry, put it in the gun and cut the end off. Clean the cow and put on your glove and lubricant. Put your arm up the cow's rectum and find the cervix through the wall of the rectum. Then put in the gun after using your elbow to pull the vulva down so you part the lips of the vulva. Guide it in so it finds the cervix. Pass it through the canal into the uterus. Press the trigger and count to five. Pull the gun out. Never use it on a cow if she's already pregnant, otherwise you endanger the unborn calf.'

Without asking permission, Pearl then resumed her place.

Of course, Pearl always had a photographic memory.

I have told you of my first memory of Pearl Wyss. Why do I mention her?

Well, Pearl played, and plays, a leading role not only in my own life, but in the life of every girl in the school.

Yes indeed, some are born great, some become great, and some have greatness thrust upon them, like money for an errand.

Perhaps it's best to face facts. Five years ago, in 1975 – Tuesday the 27th of April, in fact, at just after ten o'clock – a little something happened that you, the reader, cannot be insensible of.

At the time – just before ten o'clock – my mother, the headmistress, was taking a swimming class. The school is quite extensive, with swimming-block, gymnasium, and chapel, as well as the expected classrooms, dormitories, refectory, assembly hall *und so wieter*, and I was being treated, as was quite normal, to the sight of fifty or so girls in a state of semi-nakedness.

These fifty or so were most of the fourth form, the rest of the school having departed on two trips: the lower school to Loch Lomond, where they were making plaster casts of otter's feet in the mud, and the sixth to the Limoges region, where they were competing in a wind-band contest and being deflowered.

Swimming, I was thin, brown and fourteen; and swimming, they were fat, white and fourteen, except in the cases where they were thin, white and fourteen.

All girls wore the regulation one-piece black swimming costume and white swimming cap with daisy. I submitted to the wearing of swimming trunks. But though my trunks were e'er so tight, ne'er did I repine. We, the girls and I, had been bathing together our whole lives, and I had no very active thoughts of the potentialities imminent in their costumes.

My mother was directing operations, the two other remaining staff members – the cook and Miss Peabody, who taught German and history, a piquant combination – having departed on a day-trip to Aberdeen to stock up on something.

This was, as I say, just before ten o'clock. I should also say that the swimming block is a windowless building, the only natural illumination coming from a row of clerestory panels high up on all four walls. And perhaps the church comparison is apt, because at precisely just after ten o'clock, the swimming-hall was lit up with an extraordinary burst of pure white light, as if the Lord had chosen that moment to declare he had invented a new type of Easter and was giving a press conference about it.

The girls put their hands over their eyes and shrieked. I too was momentarily blinded, dropping to the ground at the side of the pool. The light faded. We looked around us. What had it been? My mother was comforting some of the girls nearest her. A minute passed. And then, with a hideous roar, all the windows blew in, scattering the surface of the pool in a million tiny rocks. The girls' soft shoulders and arms, abraded in a thousand places, began to bleed into the pool, turning it pink; and, as the building juddered and the girls screamed, flame poured in through the windows and a great stink of dust and tar filled our nostrils. At the deep end, a section of ceiling gave way and crashed into the water.

My mother gave a sharp blast on her whistle. 'To me!' she cried.

All fifty of us began to hobble or swim toward her: I could see May Sussums, recently the recipient of a school prize for *faux*-First-World-War poetry, distraught and sobbing; Elizabeth Pelham, supine, her hair loose, clinging to the leg of her best friend Francesca Mond, who was dragging her along; and Rowena Northcote-Heathcote, shrieking mindlessly. No girl at that point seemed to have been badly injured.

'Line up by house!' my mother commanded.

15

The girls began to get in line. There were fifty-four of them, and it came out to about fourteen per line.

'Captain of house to front of line!'

Amid the weeping, Robyn Loss-Stevenson (Captain, Brownstone), Amber Wells (Acting Captain, Wideopen), Pearl Wyss (Captain, Darling), and Mary-Dot Golding (Captain, Mancoe), moved to the front of their respective lines.

It was at this juncture, with the noise dying down and stock having been taken of the situation, and the girls beginning to calm, that my mother seemed momentarily to pause for thought. The aforementioned (some several pages ago) Yolanda Vane-Hovell-Vane – a ridiculous name but her own – who also happened to be Head of Year and Captain of Wideopen – had been excused swimming on the grounds of having won an honourable mention at an equestrian event the previous month in York, and was at that moment engaged in currying the horse. My mother had objected to this absence, on the grounds that swimming was healthful, that the horse did not need currying, and that it set a bad precedent; but Near School for Girls was nothing if not a hemi-semi-democratic institution, and the riding-mistress – at that moment in Cornwall – had prevailed in the argument. My mother had in fact confided to me the evening before: 'That horse will be the death of me.'

And so, giving the care of a swimming-pool-full of sobbing girls to no one in particular, she wrested with the double doors and strode out into the quad to see what had become of Yolanda, fastening the doors behind her with strict instructions not to open them until her return.

There was a brief lull, during which I gave myself over to a search for cuts or damage to my person. I found none. The only immediate cause for alarm seemed to be the fact that smoke now lay over the surface of the swimming-pool as if it were an Arthurian mere. But then, not more than thirty seconds after my mother's departure, and to our collective horror, a second blaze of pure white light streamed through the now deglazed upper storey. This time we knew what was coming. Many of the girls, in fear of their lives, leapt panic-stricken into the pool, seeking to escape the blast in the smoking waters. I crouched. And about a minute later the expected shock-wave came, again rending the air with saurian ferocity, while a series of smaller detonations seemed to follow in quick succession.

Blundering through the choking smoke and heat, the screams of fifty-four girls ringing in my ears, I found my way to the doors, and, in strict contravention of my mother's instructions, flung them wide. Looking past smouldering trees and grass turned black, the west side of the school was on fire. And there in the quad, spinning languidly round and round, was my mother, burning.

The two explosions, we learned much later, were both from Aberdeen. And those of us who were not too distracted would have noticed smaller concussions arriving pell-mell from other cities. Scotland, and perhaps the whole United Kingdom, was being obliterated.

I believe we endured that day and its horrors chiefly by holding fast to the idea that we would be rescued. My mother, accordingly, was left where she had fallen and breathed her last, in case the emergency services had an opinion on the subject. I lay beside her. By 3 o'clock that afternoon, her thin body was cold to the touch.

Then someone laid a sheet over her and we carried her into the school.

The school, I should say, had gone out. Things do on Near.

Yolanda – poor Yolanda – was also badly burnt, and I am afraid to say she took an hour to die. She was in great pain.

The horse survived, since it had remained in its stable. Yolanda had not been currying him after all. What she had been doing among the fruit canes is hard to say.

That day did not bring the arrival of strong men in boats, nor even puny men in coracles. In fact the day ended abruptly at about four o'clock, the skies having darkened somewhat atypically for late spring.

Have you ever witnessed the death of your own mother? Well, perhaps you have; many people have, these days. Around five o'clock, we gathered around the two corpses, laid side by side on a bench in the laboratory. The only adult and the only functioning near-adult. We were now fifty-four girls and one boy on an island in the middle of a new world in which the skies were full of ash.

On that afternoon, few had any idea what to say in the presence of the dead. I think it was Amber Wells, the new captain of Wideopen, who tentatively murmured, as we stood around the bench: 'I'm so sorry, Stephen.'

My competent and beautiful mother. But along with grief and horror came something akin to exhilaration. For the first time in my life, things really couldn't get any worse.

'Thank you,' I said, looking around at their dirty and tear-stained faces. 'My mother… my mother died trying to save Yolanda and Murray Mint. She loved you all.'

'We loved her too, Stephen!' exclaimed Alexandra Featherstonehaugh.

'Thank you Alexandra,' I said. 'I think we should do our best to stay as safe as we can and to keep going until help arrives. We have to support each other. That's what Mum would have wanted.'

And here I am afraid I burst into tears.

Naturally it unleashed an answering Niagara of female condolence. Then, after the hubbub had subsided, Pearl Wyss spoke.

Pearl, at fourteen years old, was not an awful lot bigger than she had been at twelve. Neither had she blossomed in womanly appeal. In fact she was scrawny, flat-chested and sallow, looking less like a human being than a bad painting of one. However, she was top in all subjects except sports.

'Thank you, Stephen,' she said. 'We all feel the same way about Mrs Ballantyne. But I think we must face some unpleasant facts. Number one is that I don't think anyone is coming to help us.'

'How do you know that?' Polly Findhorn asked indignantly.

'Because,' said Pearl, 'those things were atom bombs.'

'How do you know?'

'Because I don't know what else could have reached us from the mainland like that. Certainly no other type of explosive.'

We were all fourteen years old, you must remember, and so most of us were more interested in jelly tots than nuclear armaments.

'You're just guessing,' said Polly Findhorn.

'And if they were atom bombs,' Pearl continued, 'and there were at least two of them, maybe a lot more, then what has just happened is a nuclear war. And they were miles and miles away. I'd guess they were dropped on Aberdeen.'

'How could an explosion reach us from Aberdeen?' asked Camilla Moon Khan. 'It takes half the day just to get there.'

'Yes,' said Pearl. 'Well, I'm afraid that's how powerful nuclear weapons are.'

'I don't believe it,' said Melissa Verne, and actually laughed.

'Pearl's right,' said Helen Maitland. 'It could have been a hydrogen bomb.'

'And we're one of the most isolated places in Britain,' Pearl went on. 'If we were affected like this' – she gestured around her at the laboratory, with its shattered windows and debris – 'then just imagine what the rest of the country must look like.'

I think many of the girls up to that point had seen the death of my mother as regrettable, certainly, but chiefly my own affair. Yolanda had been a hard blow, but other Heads of Year would arise and flourish. They hadn't given any thought to their own families.

'What about London?' asked Titania ('Titty') Pickering.

Pearl shrugged.

'You think they're all dead, don't you?' Titty asked her. 'You think they're all burned alive.'

'I can't know for certain,' said Pearl.

'You can't know anything and you're a dwarf,' Titty said. She stalked determinedly off. A couple of girls went after her, but most stayed to listen. They were from the better parts of the best places, and they were becoming aware for the first time that those best places had been incinerated.

'So what do we do?' Eufemia Paleocapa enquired in business-like tones.

'We have to do what Stephen just mentioned,' Pearl said, glancing at me. 'We have to look after ourselves. We have to find out how much food and water we've got and start to ration it out. We have to gather more supplies where we can.'

'Like what?'

'I don't know. Wood for heating. Eggs. Rabbits.'

'Oh, God.'

'Puffins.'

'But puffins are protected!' cried Julia Fitt-Matt.

Julia was a member of the Puffin Club, and as far as I could remember there was no Puffin Cookbook.

'Seals,' said Pearl.

'I'm not eating seal,' said Beulah Gaze. 'It's all blubber.'

'And we have to try to repair some of the damage,' Pearl continued, dropping the topic. 'I believe there is a generator, but only a limited supply of fuel, and that won't last long, so we'll have to ration it out.'

Standing flanked by the twins Henrietta ('Henry') and Thomasina ('Tom') Keck, Pearl spoke firmly and slowly, looking everyone in the eye. She didn't seem to be at all put out by being called a 'dwarf'. Perhaps it was her Christian faith.

'The radio is out,' she continued. 'Henry has searched the whole dial. Nothing from Europe at all. And there's no television. At some point we'll need to find out exactly what did happen. And then we'll need to make plans for the future. Today we need to say our prayers, and go to bed.'

And so, sweeping aside fragments of broken glass, Pearl knelt by the bodies of my mother and Yolanda Vane-Hovell-Vane, while outside, a few disconsolate puffins shrieked into the gathering gloom.

'Dear God,' she said. 'Keep us safe in our hour of peril. Protect us from war and the hand of war. Give us the strength to continue through this night and those that come after. Give us the strength to labour during the day to do your will. Look after this island and those who have survived this catastrophe wrought by man. Protect us from sickness and hunger. Bring peace to the world and let war cease. For thine is the glory, the power and the glory, for ever and ever, Amen.'

Overlooking the fact that she had stolen the ending and fluffed up the last line of the Lord's Prayer, I found it a pretty good performance.

The scale of the violence was such that we were unable reasonably to respond. Were we truly the survivors of the end of the world? Was everybody really dead? What had caused it? Was it hate? Could it be that hate was so potent? Or was it indifference? Could it be that indifference was more potent than hate?

And so we were left. No teachers. No parents. No policemen. Just us, and a horse.

It is educative to see true violence: it puts everything else into perspective.

The girls spent a miserable night. Some wept themselves to sleep. Others failed to sleep at all. When morning came, we were swollen-eyed and limp-bodied.

That first morning, the immediate task was to bury the bodies of my mother and Yolanda. I dug my mother's grave myself, near an elm by the Shute Building. We placed my mother in it, wrapped in her bedspread, which featured an embroidery-work depiction of the children of the world holding hands.

Rain pattered on excavated earth. I threw in the first handful of soil. I read from a piece of paper I had found in the chapel. In fact, I had ripped the piece of paper from a prayer-book, feeling that no one would care. I think my contempt for the prayer-book was a mistake, because now I can't remember what was on the piece of paper.

Pearl spoke over the grave of Yolanda, dilating on her many virtues as Head Girl. Some of the girls cried. Simple markers were erected featuring the penwomanship of that talented calligrapher, Samara Slavens.

Then we began the assessment that Pearl had recommended. It was, at least, something to do.

In fact, the school was very well stocked. It had to be in order to supply the daily needs of a hundred and twenty girls, and it was separated from Aberdeen by a ninety-minute sea journey (by diesel-powered ferry), so this was not, perhaps, surprising.

The generator, situated in the basement, was still operational, and there were good reserves of fuel. There were freezers full of meat, poultry and fish, and in the pantry were breads, buns and cakes, cheese, butter, milk and eggs, and leguminous comestibles including apples, bananas, oranges, tangerines, lemons, pears, grapefruits, carrots, potatoes (in plenteous sackfuls), spinach, broccoli, cabbage, lettuce, brussels sprouts, corn, onions and swede. In terms of non-perishables, or less-perishables, there were the canned soups, dried soups (I told you soup was going to be important), canned beans and tomatoes, canned fish, canned meat, pickled onions, flour and rice, various bags of dried lentils, peas and beans, spaghetti, macaroni, salt, pepper, other seasonings of other ilks, sugar, honey, cocoa, dried milk, UHT milk, instant desserts and powders, nuts of the wal, Brazil and pea families, jarred and canned fruits and vegetables, chutneys and jams, tomato puree in drums, stock cubes, yeast, baking powder, mustard, vinegar, mayonnaise, oil, tea, coffee and corn flakes.

Girls who seemed fit for the task were assigned (by Henry and Tom) to work out menus prioritising the perishables, at differing rates depending on how perishable they were.

A group of other girls were asked to make an inventory of the island's animal populations, with a view to eating them. Puffins, of course, have already been mentioned: in fact, the school coat of arms featured a puffin, along with a Near Salamander (of which more later). There also a large variety of other feathered friends. The Near Islands, being a nature reserve, were known for their seabirds. Arctic terns, gulls, shags, guillemots, kittiwakes and razorbills lived there in their unmelodious thousands. Rabbits abounded (and bounded). On nearby Wideopen Island there were flotillas of grey seals. Grey seals are capital breeders. That is a technical term.

Neither would we be without eider. Eider ducks were regular visitors.

Bettina Farque and Kay Hawkins, from Wideopen and Mancoe houses respectively, were deputised to investigate the need for repair work, which, given the sorry state of the west side of the school (charred woodwork and shattered glass) was of vital concern. The workshop had, it seemed, been spared too much damage, and in it, intact, were found a variety of things that could be put to good use: nails, screws and bolts, screwdrivers, pliers, hammers and saws, hacksaws and bowsaws, three axes, an electric lawnmower of ancient vintage and little conceivable use, a plane, set squares, drills and bits, chisels, spanners, carborunda, a vice, a sledgehammer, a pickaxe, rasps and files, ladders, dozens of shovels, spades and forks (to enable classfuls of girls to garden simultaneously), pruners, rakes, wheelbarrows, pots, trays, composting bins and work-gloves. The only serious deficiency was in scrap wood for repairs, but Bettina Farque in her thorough prospectus recommended the dismantling of one of the more damaged outbuildings to procure the necessary timber.

Girls often fall over, into things, down stairs and on top of one another. The infirmary was therefore well stocked with splints, poultices, analgesics, antibiotics, plasters, bandages, salves, ointments and even a charming instrument to bite on while in labour. Alexandra Featherstonehaugh and Kat Egg, both from Mancoe, in charge of medical operations, were able to supply the requisite balms to those girls who had received cuts.

The only serious deficiency on the island was the lack of fresh water.

In fact, the problem of fresh water rather dominated those first few weeks. It's not much use making up careful menus of meat and fruit if you know you're going to die of thirst in days.

The school had always been provisioned from the mainland by a boat that carried a water-lorry. This lorry would lumber up to the school every three weeks and discharge itself noisily into our main storage tank by the dormitories. As luck would have it, the lorry's last visit had been exactly eight days ago, and during most of those eight days, fewer than half of the girls had been present at the school. This meant that it was very nearly full: there was enough water to last, not the normal three weeks, but a good six weeks – more, if we didn't take any baths and conserved all water supplies rigorously. After all, when you have boiled a pan of potatoes, you don't throw the water away, do you? Well, perhaps you do. I don't know how you live.

But six weeks, eight weeks, ten weeks, is not forever. So on the third day after the disaster, a meeting was convened in the assembly hall.

Bee Wasket appeared to be chairing the meeting on this occasion. She was an intimidating young woman who was fond of getting other girls into headlocks. (For me, she reserved a special sort of goading. I remember sitting behind her in French. During a lull in the lesson she turned around and said to me: 'You'll never understand, Stephen. The blood.' I had absolutely no idea what she was talking about.)

'The agenda here,' Bee said, 'is about water. What are we going to do about water?'

Silence. A smell of burnt paint and scorched wood. Duenna Gee stood up. 'Can we drink sea-water?'

'No,' Bee said. 'It's poisonous.'

'What about desalination?' Duenna asked.

Bee frowned.

Pearl stood up. 'I've had a quick look in the library, and I think desalination would be difficult on a large scale. It requires quite a bit of energy. The obvious way to do it would be by distillation, which would involve boiling the water and collecting the steam, but that takes a lot of fuel. Of course it *would* be possible, if we're desperate.'

'All right,' said Bee. 'Any other ideas?'

'It's obvious,' said Titty Pickering. 'Drink the swimming-pool.'

'It's full of crap,' said Bee. 'Also it's got chlorine in it. You'd puke.'

Ludivine Nockolds stood up. She was the daughter of a Breton actress and a Yorkshire hill-farmer, and wanted to be a meteorologist. 'It precipitates here,' she said. 'We get a lot of precipitation from the North Sea. It precipitates when it hits the islands.'

'Christ,' said Bee.

'It does!' said Ludivine. Just think about it. If we put down a big collecting sheet, we can have all the water we want.'

Convinced by the meteorological ineluctability of her argument, she sat down.

Pearl stood up. 'I think the problem with that is that we might get ill. There could be radiation in the water.'

'How do you know that?' asked Ludivine.

'There's just been a nuclear war,' Pearl said.

Ludivine failed to say anything else for the rest of this book.

'What else is there?' asked Bee.

'Has anyone heard anything on the radio?' asked Jessica Robinson.

'Let's keep to the script,' said Bee. 'Anyway, you heard what she said. They're all dead.'

Pearl stood up again. 'I've thought about this, and I think we have two options. The first is simple water traps.'

'What are they?' asked Bee.

'You make a hole and put salt water in it in pots. Then you stretch a piece of plastic sheet over the hole with a dip in the middle, and put an empty pot under it. The salt water evaporates and water-drops form on the underside of the plastic. Then they drip into the pot. But that would mean digging a lot of traps. Maybe it could work – I've never tried.'

'What's the second option?'

'To dig. Deep down.'

'Why?' asked Bee.

'This island is mainly chalk. There's a chance there's fresh water down there. We have the tools. We've got nothing to lose.'

'Who's in favour?' asked Bee.

A few hands fluttered uncertainly up.

'What about your other idea?' Polly Findhorn asked. 'I mean the water traps. They sound a lot easier.'

'We can do both,' said Pearl. We can have a team on the traps, and a team on the digging. Meanwhile we'll conserve what we have.'

'All in favour?' asked Bee. Hands went up. She counted. 'I make it twenty-nine. That's a majority.'

At this point I think I should mention Albert. You will remember Albert. My pipit. That fateful day I'd left him in my room as usual. When I finally went back to it, that terrible night of that fateful day, he had gone.

There had of course been a thermonuclear war, so the disappearance of a small brown bird was not surprising. But given that my room was more or less undamaged by the series of world-ending blasts, where was he? I looked on the floor, around the room, in the drawers; I tidied up the room, putting papers and books back in order. I straightened the wall-clock. Still no Albert.

The door had not been left open; nor had the windows; the room had no chimney. The mystery was of Sherlockian proportions. There was no way he could have got out. Had the door flown open, Albert decamped, and then someone shut it?

I made enquiries, but Albert's disappearance, while sad, could not rank as tragedy. There were other things to think about.

I was on the trap team, along with Deedee Foe, Alice Celia Swash and Helen Maitland.

Deedee Foe was tall, helpful and mature; Alice Celia Swash dreamed of money; and Helen Maitland's parents were nudists.

The way to make a water trap, as Pearl had outlined, is not so complicated. First you dig a hole about a foot and a half deep. In it you put three bowls or cans of seawater ranged around the sides of the hole. In the middle you put a larger pot, empty. Then you cover the hole with a sheet of plastic and cover the edges of the plastic with earth to seal it tight. In the centre of the plastic sheet you put a small stone, creating a downward cone. Then you wait. The idea is that a little cycle of evaporation and condensation takes place in the sealed microcosm of the hole. What goes up, must come down.

Water vapour leaves the sea-water as pure H20, condenses on the underside of the sheet, and runs down towards the nadir of the inverted cone, dripping into the main basin. Even if water later evaporates from said main basin, there is no escape for it. It must condense on the underside of the sheet and return to its origin. Simple and neat. Unfortunately it didn't work very well.

It was May, and not a very warm May. Grey cloud, thick and grimy, layer on layer, prohibited any view of sun, moon or stars. Had we been Babylonians at the dawn of civilisation trying to work out our place in the cosmos, those erratically wandering planets that inspired the beginnings of science would have been invisible. Luckily we were not at the dawn of civilisation. We were at the dusk. Such were our consolations.

So there was no sun. It was rainy and chilly. In fact it was mildly embarrassing. The water traps did trap water, but it was rainwater, and it was on the wrong side of the sheet, i.e. the top. Forming little puddles.

After a day, we uncovered our first trap and found a basin almost entirely unvisited by the right sort of water. Moreover, when we tried the few drops that had collected there, they were distinctly brackish.

Later improvements to the technique did achieve some results, and after a week, we were not ready to call it an abject failure, having collected about a pint from sixteen traps. But a pint over a week cannot keep fifty-four girls and one boy from dying of dehydration. And how could such a plan work in the winter? The bowls would freeze over.

'Perhaps if it were scaled up by a factor of a hundred,' Pearl said, pursing her lips. 'It's possible we could use a heat source. Maybe put hot stones into the holes.'

The well-digging seemed to hold an equally scanty share of promise.

The well-diggers were a team of six: Melissa Verne, Sam Keller, Patsy Hugenoth, Lettice Fine, Tom Keck and Maud Colby, all from Darling House, of which Pearl was the captain.

A spot was chosen near the dorms.

The work was at first quite easy. Soon the hole, around five and a half feet in diameter, had been excavated to a depth of about a yard. Two girls worked for a 30-minute shift before being relieved, the remaining four either resting or bucketing away spoil.

The soil was loamy at the top and chalky-loamy beneath, composed of a mixture of native soil (the islands must, in the distant past, have been forested, before being denuded and then re-forested), chalk and guano.

No water, however, was in evidence.

By the third day the diggers were now in the hole up to the crowns of their unclean heads, and it became necessary to begin removing the spoil by rope-borne bucket. The soil was then carried to a growing tell some eight yards off.

By the fourth day, the well had been dug to a depth of ten feet, and the girls' hands, even though gloved, were blistered. Fresh girls were supplied from various houses: Fritzi Pietsch from Hamm (or Fritzi Hamm from Pietsch), Henry Keck, Amber Wells, Zillah Smith and yours truly (though not, strictly speaking, a girl). The hole was now accessed via a ladder.

On the sixth day the guano gave out, and the loam. At twelve feet we struck bedrock. And still no sign of water.

Please take a moment to imagine a hole twelve feet deep. That is a very deep hole. When you looked at the diggers from above, they were as if seen from a first-floor window, toiling there in the chalk-illumined dark.

Pearl came to inspect the diggings. Our morale was low. Lettice Fine, a flautist, was worried about the damage to her fingers. Patsy Hugenoth, who had plans concerning international jet-setting, was covered in dirt.

'This is excellent,' Pearl said. 'You've got to the rock. And it's chalk. Imagine if you'd found granite. Aberdeen is famous for its granite, you know. We'd be stumped. But Near is made of soft sedimentary rock. Actually, believe it or not, you're at sea level already. This part of the island is only twelve feet above sea level. And still no sea-water. That's encouraging. It means the chalk isn't saturated. The water-table, when you get to it, might well be fresh. Use the pick from now on. Going will be much slower but the sides will be more stable. If you can excavate around two inches day, that makes over a foot a week, or four feet a month. Don't give up. We're all counting on you. The race is not to the swift, nor the battle to the strong.'

Personally I was dubious. The race usually *is* to the swift, and the battle usually *is* to the strong. And where would the water come from? Were there freshwater rivers flowing down there? Surely not. We were thirteen miles from the mainland. But I kept my doubts to myself.

If you eternally hope for springs, hope springs eternal.

In any case, the girls needed something to keep their minds occupied.

We now held meetings every morning in the assembly hall. The windows on the west side had been boarded up and we were dependent on light from the east, there being no electricity. The rubble and dust had been cleared away and the floor mopped with seawater mixed with cleaning fluid.

Many and varied issues were discussed. Camilla Moon Khan wished to know what had really happened. The primal question, one might say. Laura Huxley wondered how we could get to the mainland and whether we should build a boat; Michaela Kodiak raised the question of tides. Pamela Gowler and Joy Sadd asked whether we should continue with lessons. Titty Pickering said that lessons had never helped anybody before and they were unlikely to do so now. Rowena Northcote-Heathcote wondered who was in charge of repairs because the window near her bed had a piece missing. Sam Keller asked whether anyone had read *The Swiss Family Robinson*, and whether there were any useful tips in it.

Melissa Verne and Char Parr brought up the question of the vegetable garden, and whether or not it was radioactive. The consensus was that it might be a little radioactive. Julia Fitt-Matt claimed that if the vegetables were radioactive, then the seabirds were also radioactive, and that we should not then eat them. May Sussums wondered whether it was possible to 'catch' radioactivity. She was laughed at.

Kay Hawkins said that May might have a point, and actually – was it possible? And was laughed at.

Various girls speculated on how long you can last with radioactivity before you die, and how you know whether you've got it or not. Robyn Loss-Stevenson said that radioactivity was not something you 'got'. You were exposed to it. A short debate ensued on what the difference was, if any.

The possibility of rescue was again raised. No data being available, the discussion turned to the washing of clothes, and whether it was possible in seawater. Robyn said that seawater was composed of water and minerals. Patsy Hugenoth asked what would happen when we ran out of soap, and Anne Heaviside asked whether, if you hang clothes out to dry, they become radioactive.

Eunice Riddley wondered how much electricity we had left, and Samara Slavens asked if we could make electricity. This led to a discussion about candles. Fritzi Pietsch from Hamm (or Fritzi Hamm from Pietsch) said that she had once made candles, and it wasn't difficult as long as you had wax and a box of wicks. Tom Keck and Kat Egg returned to the subject of washing, this time personal cleansing, and the suitability of seawater.

Beulah Gaze asked whether the sun was ever going to come out again. Barbara Pulmow apologised for interrupting and said that she had asthma and didn't know what she was going to do when she ran out of salbutamol. Bettina Farque interrupted this by asking whether the war was actually over, or whether it was going to start again, and if it was over, who'd won, and if we'd won, whether that made any difference.

Emma-Jane Crotch wondered where Albert was. I was unable to enlighten her. Lisa Plast asked about mealtimes. These had been organised so far on an ad hoc basis, with Elizabeth Pelham (who had long hair she was proud of) as quartermistress, but it was clear we needed more managerial input.

Francesca Mond asked if the spelling contest was cancelled. Deedee Foe asked who should write down the minutes, and it was decided that I should do it.

Several of the more important questions were selected for a debate. The result was passed to a council of elected members for implementation. The council consisted of the four house captains and their deputies.

One of the liveliest debates concerned the slaughter and consumption of Murray Mint.

The resolution in this case was: 'This house proposes that Murray Mint be slaughtered and eaten.'

The debate took place on the second Saturday after the end
of the world, in the assembly hall. Titty Pickering proposed the
resolution, with Minna Bye seconding. Julia Fitt-Matt opposed
it, with Gabby Tate seconding.

It was about eleven o'clock in the morning. It had been
raining all night and the air inside the school smelled of mud.

'Murray Mint,' said Titty, 'is essentially pointless. He's only
used for recreation. We can't afford him. If he was slaughtered,
he could feed fifty girls for five months.'

'Point of information,' said Mickey Kodiak, placing her
hand on top of her head.

'Granted,' said Harriet Gupping in the chair.

'Where did you get those figures from?'

Titty took a long time conferring with Minna. 'They're
approximate figures,' she said at last, 'based on Murray Mint's
approximate weight.'

'Point of information,' repeated Mickey.

'Not granted,' said Harriet.

'If you really want to know,' said Titty, 'we estimate his
weight at about a ton, and half of that is unusable, being
internal organs and things. So that's about a half a ton of meat.
If a girl eats a pound of meat a week, there are about one
thousand one hundred pounds in a half a ton, so that means
about a thousand weeks for one girl, or twenty weeks for fifty
girls. Twenty weeks is five months. And that's just one horse.'

'It would go off!' shouted someone at the back.

'Thank you, Titty,' said Harriet, looking green. I knew for a
fact that Harriet dreamt about the most expensive chocolates
in the world, and here we were talking about rotting horsemeat.

Julia Fitt-Matt took the floor. 'I'm sorry,' she said, 'but how
do you know if he weighs a ton? Have you got a scale? I bet it's
a lot less than that. Anyway, Murray Mint might have uses we
haven't thought of yet. And we can't bring him back from the

dead if we change our minds. Besides, it's inhumane. And you might kill him and then find he's so tough you can't eat him. Napoleon ate his horse but only after he'd run out of everything else.'

'Point of information,' said Deedee Foe, placing her hand on her head.

'Granted,' said Harriet.

'Napoleon didn't eat his horse. It survived and lived in Paris. His soldiers ate their horses because an army marches on its stomach.'

'Anything with a stomach,' said Julia, 'marches on its stomach. Murray Mint survived the explosion just like we did and we should look after him. Anyway, I'm a vegetarian so I don't believe in eating animals.'

Not many of the girls were vegetarians, so this last point was not really an appeal to a broad constituency. But Julia sat down with a certain emphasis.

Minna then seconded Titty, leaning heavily on the sheer waste of resources embodied in the equine. Gabby rebutted Minna by saying that his manure was good for the garden. Finally, each principal speaker was given the opportunity to rebut the opposing pair's arguments and to sum up her case. The school then voted.

'For the motion, five,' said Harriet. 'Opposing the motion, thirty-five. So the resolution is defeated.'

A cheer went up. Murray Mint, though his very name connoted edibility, was saved. This later proved to be a very good thing.

In any case, it was difficult to imagine even Titty felling Murray Mint with an axe.

I say 'even Titty'. Was Titty, then, nearly capable of such an act?

Perhaps. Whatever the case, I confess I found her irresistible. She was so wrong about everything.

Titty was from Mancoe House. She was sharp-nosed, severe, and rarely laughed. Her reaction to humour was a goat-faced stare. She wore large black-rimmed glasses, which were often set crooked. Her face, covered in freckles, was like a negative map of the heavens. I have said there were no longer stars in our world. That is not precisely true. How I longed to devise new constellation-maps from the glowing suns of her skin.

She played the clarinet, carrying it in a chunky blue box with metal corners that made my heart pound. I envied that clarinet, nestling in its red plush; I envied it as it was taken out and fitted together so sweetly.

Titty, however, seemed entirely uninterested in me. It was brutally unfair. I was the only boy in the school. And I was not a freak. Just a little small and pontifical. What did she want out of life? A fat man with a moustache?

I *had* talked to her a couple of times – once when she dropped a stack of maths books and I picked them up for her. I don't think she said 'thank you'. The second time was when I happened to be wandering in a corridor near the dorms (I roomed with my mother in the Shute Building) and passed her. She asked haughtily: 'Are you lost?' To which I replied: 'No, I'm just walking round and round in circles.' 'Well, don't get dizzy,' she said.

It seemed to me – it still seems – that there is a perfect riposte to this, but I have never been able to think what it is.

It's curious: I take a practical approach to life. A boy with less of an inclination to take advantage of a half-ruined school full of unruined girls is difficult to imagine. In most cases I would rather curl up with a good book.

But Titty was an exception. Who knows why? There were girls in the school with far straighter glasses.

Titty Pickering. So deliciously silly a name.

Stephen and Titty. Stephen and Titty Ballantyne are invited to dinner at 7pm at the Smiths'. Bring a bottle.

But there are no Smiths, and 7pm or no 7pm, there is work to do, repairing classrooms, washing clothes, cooking meals, digging holes.

After the second week we were at thirteen feet. A log had now been set up on one side, staked in position so we could run the rope over it to bring up the buckets.

A girl would drop a plumb line into the void after every three shifts to ascertain if the hole were true – that is, following a strict vertical course.

The pair at the bottom were now relieved every twenty minutes, and the entire team had expanded, with the addition of Henry Keck, Jules Cashford and Anne Baring. Work tended to proceed only when the sun was well up – though it never broke through the clouds – because it was only during the lighter portions of the day that we could see what in the name of Lucifer we were doing.

The third Thursday after the war I was in the hole with Zillah, a strapping young woman with braces on her teeth. A distinctly sub-par student, Zillah was ideally suited to swinging a pickaxe at the bottom of a hole. In fact she made me nervous. I felt like Leon Trotsky. Was the bottom of that hole my Mexico?

'You've got to hand it to Pearl,' Zillah grunted, swinging. 'Did you hear her this morning? She's building a Khyber counter.'

'Geiger counter,' I said. 'Yes, she…'

'Get that,' she said, pointing to some chalk spoil.

I obliged. 'I don't think she's building one, exactly,' I said. 'She just asked Robyn to look into building one. I don't think it's actually possible.'

'Yes, but that's the thing about Pearl,' Zillah interrupted. She lifted the pick. 'She says that things which seem impossible' – the pick landed murderously – 'can be done if you do them bit by bit.'

I could smell her sweat. It was a chlorine-like reek. In fact I could smell her rather more distinctly than I could see her.

'One thing she *did* say,' I said carefully, 'is that we shouldn't go over the bounds of the plumb line.'

Zillah stopped swinging and straightened up, resting the pick-head on the ground, one hand on her hip. 'Who's doing this, you or me?' she asked.

'You,' I said.

'Then let's get on with it. What we need here is some muscle.'

Shouldering the instrument once more, she let fly, but instead of hitting the ground, the point landed meatily in the wall of the chamber. There was a short pause while Zillah, grunting, withdrew it. A little trickle of gravel and chalk followed. And then, as we watched in horror, a substantial mass of earth and rock, about eighteen inches in diameter, spat itself rudely from the side of the wall. Zillah and I took a couple of steps back. We could hear something. A noise like a grumbling or groaning, as if the earth were ill at ease and wished to make itself comfortable. Then, with a hideous crack, six feet of wall broke away just above our heads and slid down on top of us. We were suddenly buried up to our waists, pinned against the opposite wall. Something big had fallen on my foot. The pain was excruciating.

'Help!' Zillah cried. 'Help!'

There were answering cries from above. Soon two ropes came snaking down. We grasped them and pulled. But however much we pulled, we could not pull free.

Maud Colby's face appeared at the top of the well. 'Wait there!' she shouted.

A little bubble of hysteria forced itself up from my chest. Zillah regarded me with horror.

'We're going to die,' she whimpered. 'Why are you laughing?'

'She said "Wait there".'

Zillah looked like a cat who has heard a dog on the radio. Then she too began to laugh. '"Wait there"?' She began to sob. '"Wait there".'

Maud Colby reappeared, her face like a teacup. 'OK, we've got all the girls on the ropes. Tie the ropes tightly under your arms. We're going to pull you free. There are ten of us. We'll get you out. Okay?'

'Okay!' I shouted. I made myself a quick under-arm harness, then supervised a similar one for Zillah.

'Done it?' shouted Maud.

'Yes!'

'I don't know who has which rope, so we're going to do this one first!'

'Okay!'

It was evidently Zillah's rope, because with a squawk she flew up out of the ground, bashing into the side of the well and into space. It was rather like seeing a girl falling into a well, only in reverse. She disappeared into the light and was dragged over the lip of the well and out of sight. Chalk and earth moved with resentful thuddings to fill the void where she had been. Was that noise the same groaning, grumbling? Cracking?

'Get me out of here!' I screamed.

'Okay! Go!' shouted Maud. And, with a prodigious yank, I found myself rising out of my tomb, limbs flailing. In moments my head was poking up over the lip of the well, and my hands were seizing mud and lawn.

Ten filthy seraphim chorused at the top of their lungs. 'Hooray for Stephen!'

Zillah was lying unconscious on the grass a little way off.

Pearl came to inspect the workings. 'We should have reinforced the sides,' she said. 'Thank God no one was injured.'

She gazed for a while at the heap of spoil at the bottom of the hole.

'Okay, we'll do it with planks,' she continued. 'Two by two. They can be bent round to fit. They'll brace against each other and give good protection from future cave-ins. Bettina can help us with the wood. It needs to be strong but flexible. So, to start with, we'll send down one digger at a time to remove the spoil from the cave-in, and make sure she's always harnessed so she can be pulled up at a moment's notice. I'd say it's about two or three cubic yards. The ladder's too short now anyway and it'll just get in the way, so we'll lower you in and pull you up by rope each time. We'll need a really good harness that can support a person's weight comfortably, like a parachute harness. Any volunteers for that? All right, Jules. We'll ask Pam to come in on the digging team. We'll have to start casing at the bottom and then back-fill the area where the spoil has slipped down. That will equalise the pressure. When we've cased it all the way up we'll start excavating again, a bit at a time, before setting in the next ring of wood. Okay. Now, we need to make some changes. I think an improved hoist, especially since we'll be pulling you up as well as the spoil. We need to set up spars like two X's on either side of the well-head, so that the crux of each X is at about chest height. Then we'll run a beam across them, and run the rope over the beam. That means that when we're pulling, we're pulling horizontally, which will make it easier for lots of pullers working on the same rope. And it'll be easier to get to the bucket or the digger, which will just dangle free over the top of the well. There can be a platform on one side so the digger can step onto it. Well done, Stephen.'

I was nursing a sore foot but nothing seemed to be broken. Except my heart, for Titty.

I suppose I had been in love with Titty for years. I had never told a soul. It was a constant torment.

My love affair was complicated by the fact that another girl, Alison Barclay-Coutts, whose parents were both named after banks, was also in love with Titty. Such passionate attachments were not uncommon at the school.

Alison was a forlorn creature. Whereas Titty had the knack of doing everything wrong and appearing to be right, Alison had the knack of doing everything right and appearing to be wrong. She was a tall girl with hacked hair and mild eyes, and I once saw her carefully writing the following sign: 'The library is closed until opening time.'

Alison thought herself a poet, and every year produced a book of verse that she exhibited at the school fair. It never won a prize. How can an exercise book hope to compete with a life-size papier-mâché Tutankhamun?

Miss Guss, who taught English and chemistry, was baffled by Alison. Alison appeared to have imbibed every one of Miss

Guss's exhortations on the beauty and necessity of poetry ('poets are the true legislators of the Earth') while producing verse without a shred of either.

Titty did not show any signs of returning Alison's love, which should have been a comfort to me. It wasn't. In pre-war days, secretly rifling Titty's pigeonhole at night, on more than one occasion I found messages that Alison had left, which tended to be along the lines of 'I hope your cough has cleared up. I know some really good medicine for coughs, and if you want some, I can get it really easily, you only have to ask.'

Alison suffered a downfall that was at least as shattering to her as the later destruction of Western civilisation and the elimination of her family in Cheam.

As I say, no one read her poetry, which dealt with subjects such as societal anomie, the endangerment of the world's megafauna, poetry itself, and so on. Perhaps I was her only audience. Perhaps I felt that in reading her lines I would somehow learn my own fate. Perhaps I felt that Alison's poetry would help me avoid becoming Alison.

However, one poem, entitled 'In the Wood', induced more than the ordinary ennui. The lines seemed barely to belong to one another:

Tell me where the wild wood grows, and
I will meet you there,
There beneath a bank of violets blooming,
Tired eyes wilting,
Youth drowses away the hours
In summer's prison of heat.
Lest you forget,
Or never knew in the first place,
Violets are the flowers of devotion,
Especially white violets.

Yet actually violets come in three colours:
Orange, blue and white,
Unless I am mistaken.

I do not lay claim to any poetic ability. Neither can I make a table. Yet I know if one of the legs fails to reach the floor. Some odd aroma seemed to emanate from this offering. Suddenly I saw why. The poem was an acrostic: the initial letters of each line spelled out the words 'TITTY I LOVE YOU.'

Remarkable girl! I felt almost sorry for her. The poem had been exhibited to *la toute Near* over the course of a week, to children, siblings, parents, governors, honoured donors, and anyone else who cared to leaf past it, and no one had noticed.

What to do with this information? Tell Titty herself? I was too craven for that. Tell Alison, and blackmail her? Pointless, really: she had nothing I wanted. Leak the information to the whole school? Perfect. This, then, I did, through the medium of Minna Bye. Minna Bye shared Titty's penchant for being wrong. On this occasion, however, she would be right.

I was present when Titty cornered Alison in the refectory at morning break. Titty waved the book of poems at her, ripped untimely from the exhibition in the Shute Building.

'Is this yours?' she asked.

'Yes,' Alison said humbly.

'Is it some kind of a joke?'

Alison knit her brows. The surrounding girls giggled.

'What makes you think,' Titty continued, 'that you can use my name in your stupid scribbles?'

Alison remained mute.

'Do you think my name's funny? Is that it?' asked Titty.

'No,' whimpered Alison. 'It's a nice name. I didn't mean anything. It was...' Her voice sank to a whisper. 'It was an accident.'

An unconvincing ploy.

Titty stared through glasses cocked in anger. 'What are you talking about, you stupid giraffe?'

'I wrote it by accident,' whispered Alison.

'So you wrote "Titty I love you" by accident. You must think I'm stupid!'

'No...' said Alison.

'I don't let anyone write about me unless I want them to!' said Titty, rather magisterially.

'I...'

'Using someone's name without their permission is a breach of copyright!'

Every human being has a soul. Alison's soul was being prodded with red-hot forks. She was roasting like an earwig on a burning log. The person she loved most in the world was telling her she was worthless, and she had no choice but to believe it.

Titty then did something that surprised me. She ripped the offending poem out of the book. 'Here!' she said, thrusting it in Alison's face. 'Eat it!'

Not even my wildest nightmares had prepared me for this. I felt both pity and terror – pity for Alison and terror for myself. Perhaps Titty would start on me next. Perhaps that's what love was: the infinite extension of pain.

'Eat it!' Titty screamed again.

'Eat it! Eat it! Eat it! Eat it!' chanted the watching girls.

Alison reached for the torn page, took it tremblingly, and inserted a corner between her lips. Then her face crumpled and she burst into sobs.

I longed to take back what I had done. How I wished I could stop the burning waves of hate! How I wished I could stand up and say: 'It was me! I wrote it!' Or: 'Poor never-read poetess! What harm does her love do?' Or: 'You think you've been made a fool of? How much worse never to have been loved!'

But I couldn't. Instead I said nothing and watched Alison weep.

Titty threw the book down, turned, and walked off. The book sprawled on the floor where it had fallen, soaking up the spilled cocoa of a late breakfaster.

In fact, I couldn't see afterwards why I'd done it at all. It was obvious that Alison wasn't getting anywhere with Titty. She was no threat.

I look back on it now – from six years on – and it seems one of the very worst things I have ever done. And yet I didn't mean it to turn out like that. I meant to expose Alison to Titty's contempt, not to her fury.

Dearest Alison. I injured you terribly, and no one ever knew. Everyone thought Minna had discovered the acrostic. And Minna did not disabuse them. Minna, who had never heard of an acrostic, and was hungry for notoriety.

Minna was a strange character. Nearly a victim, she had somehow found her way into being a bully. Without Titty to toady to, Minna's powerlessness and friendlessness would have been all too readily apparent; and the other girls, in a twinkling, would have stolen her pencil-case or sent her to Coventry.

Coventry is the least loquacious place in Britain. All those who are sent there, burdened with shame, cast down their eyes, and to their fellow victims utter not a word.

Pearl's plan to reinforce the side of the well with planks was, on the face of it, good. But the best-laid plans of mice and men gang aft agley.

(I think 'agley' might be fairly applied to the state of global civilisation at this point. A smoking radioactive wasteland is somewhat 'agley', all things considered.)

'The wood's too thick,' said Bettina. 'We can't bend it. It'll splinter.'

'What have you got?' asked Pearl.

'Well, we've got these bits and these bits.'

The reader cannot see the bits, so I will reveal that they were thick planks, on the one hand, and thin planks, on the other.

'I see,' said Pearl. 'Unfortunately, the thin bits won't hold the earth in.'

'But that's all we have,' said Bettina. 'Unless you want to dismantle the school.'

Pearl looked at her as if this was not entirely out of the question. 'How do you bend planks?' she mused aloud to herself.

I suppose this is the curse of us lesser mortals – we recoil from the hideous expense of time and effort involved in doing the impossible. We are easily dispirited by failure, especially in advance.

It turns out that the way you bend nine-foot planks, so as to fit in pairs, barrel-wise, into a five-and-a-half-foot diameter hole (circumference = pi times D) is by using a tea urn, some logs, a piece of garden hose and a wooden box.

How? Well, first make a box ten feet long, eighteen inches wide and eighteen inches high. A sort of ten-foot coffin for a very tall, thin man. You can do this quite simply with scrap wood. Then get the tea urn and auger a hole in the side, near the top. Make the hole slightly smaller than the diameter of the hose so that when you pass the hose into the hole it fits snugly. Drill a similar hole at one end of the ten-foot box and pass the other end of the hose into the box. Drill a second hole, low down at the other end of the box. Now place the planks to be bent in the box. Seal it up. Fill the tea urn with water. Salt water, naturally. Place a lid on the tea urn. Put the urn on an iron frame made of a garden gate supported on bricks, and put logs underneath. Set fire to the logs. The water boils and the steam passes into the ten-foot box, which acts as a steaming chamber. Do this for most of the day. At the end of the day, remove the hot salty planks (gloves, girls!) and take them to a part of the garden where stakes have been specially prepared in the shape of a five-and-a-half-foot diameter circle. Bend the hot planks around the stakes, locking them in place. Each nine-foot plank (actually trimmed a little shorter: C=pi D) makes a semicircle, and butts up against its fellow. Take a rope and connect each end of the plank down through the centre of the circle to its opposite end, for extra compressive strength. Leave overnight. In the morning, release the plank-ring from the stakes. Take it to the well and install it. Repeat.

Could you do as much, gentle reader, were you on an island?

My father was a capable man, or so my mother told me. He trained as a restorer. That requires patience, fine motor control, a certain wile with materials, a strategic mind. But I wonder if he could have bent planks with a tea-urn.

My father. Is he dead? Did he ever know about me? Probably not. I adjudge he did the deed and was off in a trice. (A trice being, in my imagining, a sort of Spanish seagoing vessel, *bien sûr*.)

I mentioned, some time ago, the subject of washing – that is, washing the body. Well, certain strictures were now in place. In brief, we all had to wash in the sea.

Or at least in sea water. Not necessarily by picking our way down a slimy beach: a pot of the stuff carried to a private location would do.

Any other decision would have been madness. We had a small supply of fresh water and it was going to run out in a few months. By Christmas we would all be eating radioactive snow. How could we use our precious fresh water for something as frivolous as washing, when we were surrounded by salt water that would do perfectly well?

Anyone opposing the decision might as well have been saying that we should die of thirst a month earlier than necessary.

Nevertheless, certain of the girls actually did oppose it. I remember the hands: Beulah Gaze, Eufemia Paleocapa, Rowena Northcote-Heathcote. It seems there are some people in this world who would rather die of thirst and face their Maker properly scrubbed than subsist a few weeks longer by dousing themselves with a bucket of freezing ocean.

If one believes in a Lord with a sensitive nose, I suppose it makes sense.

As for soap, a severe shortfall was discovered: only about a dozen bars remained. Detergent, toothpaste and shampoo were at similarly low levels. We were evidently towards the end of our supply cycle.

The remaining bars of soap had to be rationed. Each house was given three bars, under the protection of a soap-monitor. The soap-monitor could lend a bar to any girl once every five days, and had to make sure it was not returned excessively diminished in size. But with each house containing an average of thirteen and a half girls, all of them eager to exercise their washing privileges, and each five-ounce bar diminishing at a rate of .04 ounces per wash, how long would the three bars last?

Please give the answer to the nearest two significant figures.

The well was now fifteen feet deep and three feet below sea-level. It was a rather pleasing creation. Impressively buttressed with curving planks, dead straight down, it looked from within rather like an inside-out packet of wine gums.

Still no water, however.

One day around six weeks after the war, we were towards the middle of a day's work. Girls worked below, solo – a safety procedure that Pearl had introduced – while the rest of us waited up top, with buckets and rope. At least six were required up top at all times – another safety procedure – to ensure a digger could be extracted rapidly in an emergency.

We waited. I mused. The pick thudded dankly. The bucket scraped. The weather was chilly, and I was looking forward to going back down.

Every so often we would pull up a girl. It was really a girl-mine.

Sam Keller was let down. Sam was one of the girls I liked most. Her father had died when she was ten.

In the sky, clouds roiled. A grey and listless May. The world waited for warmth.

My mind turned once again to Albert. It was very perplexing. Had someone stolen him? I was beginning to incline towards the theory. But who would do such a thing? Titty? Of course not. Titania cared not a whit for me: to her, I was not even Bottom. Pearl? She had too much else to think about. Jules Cashford? Jules was a known cynic who professed an interest in the occult, and I had never trusted her. Oddly, she was, like Julia Fitt-Matt, also a vegetarian. Was Albert being used in some vegetarian Satanic rite?

I missed him. I remembered how much pleasure it had given me to heal him with nothing more than a couple of matchsticks and an elastic band. I thought of the little nubbin where the leg had calloused over. I felt again his tiny claws in my shoulder, a shoulder which was often, I regret to say, somewhat malodorous. I generally kept a cloth there, which I could wash. Teenage girls are strange about excrement.

'Water!' shrieked Sam Keller. 'Water!'

We rushed to the well-head. From below came a spitting noise like a faulty tap.

'Quickly! Quickly! Pull me up!'

We grabbed the rope. In seconds Sam was at ground level, leaping onto the platform, still holding the pick. She threw it aside and rushed into the pack of waiting girls. The bottom half of her skirt was darkly soaked.

'It's water!' she squealed, holding her skirt. 'Water! I hit the bottom and it caved in! There's loads of it down there! It just came bubbling out!'

Patsy Hugenoth threw herself on dirty knees. She grabbed Sam's skirt with both hands, bunched up the material and squeezed. She thrust her head forward, mouth open, pink tongue straining. She smacked her lips.

'It's water!' she cried in exaltation.

'Of course it's water!'

'I mean it's fresh water! It's not salty! Taste it!'

The girls knelt before Sam. They took her skirt in their mouths. 'It's fresh!' they screamed. 'It's fresh!'

I grabbed some of the skirt and squeezed. I brought my palm to my mouth and licked.

Down there, beneath Near, rainwater had collected over eons, filtered through pine needles and bracken, turf and chalk. A basin of fresh water, protected from the sea by a sloping barrier of rock. And Pearl had somehow intuited its existence. She had done what generations of monks, farmers, bird-watchers and school governors had failed to do. Just a few yards below them, all that time.

Not the digging of it, nor the reinforcing of it – she was too weak and small – but the idea of it, the planning, the persistence, was Pearl's. And now the success. Our own water, forever. A citadel on Near, entire in itself.

Without Pearl we would be dead. An odd fact.

Two

Joy Sadd saw it first: a rowboat, with a man in it. He must have rowed for miles.

As he drew nearer, girls gathered to meet him. A man. Doing what men can do. Battling, striving. Imposing himself.

Of course, I was a man too. I was fifteen, but I was a man. Or a potential man.

He rowed the boat to the weedy shore and vaulted into the water. He seized a rope at the prow and pulled the boat up beyond the reach of the waves. How had he rowed all that way? Were the tides in his favour? No one knew about tides. We had always travelled to the island by ferry.

He was a man of medium height, strong-looking, about thirty years old. Twice our age, anyway. He had brief sandy hair, an inch or so of beard, and a smile. When the boat was at rest, he did something unexpected: he knocked on the hull with his hand.

'Knock, knock!' he said, looking at the waiting crowd. 'Can I come in?'

No one answered. Walking toward us, he stopped a few feet away. 'I'm Fisher,' he said.

No one spoke.

'I'm from the mainland. Do you know what happened there?'

'Yes, a war,' said Pamela. She looked very small. She played piano, flute and oboe. That was unusual – two woodwind instruments.

'Yes,' he said. 'People died. In the cities. The cities are all gone. In the countryside there's no food. People are starving. The sun doesn't come out. It was a nuclear war. The Russians.'

Pearl stepped forward. 'What happened to the Russians?' she asked.

The man laughed. 'Who cares about the Russians? They're the ones who did this to us.'

'What about Bangladesh?' asked Camilla Moon Khan.

The man seemed to take the question seriously. 'I don't know, love. Maybe it's okay. There's no news. We know Europe's the same as here. Paris, gone. Think about that. No more Eiffel Tower.'

Several of us had actually been to the Eiffel Tower during a school trip to France a few years earlier. I can't say I'd enjoyed it much.

'Are you all girls here?' he asked, looking directly at me.

'What do you want?' Pearl asked before I could reply.

'The people on the mainland,' the man said, 'they knew you were here. They were worried about you. So we decided to send someone. I drew the short straw.' He smiled.

The speech was remarkable in that it contained three pronouns: 'They', 'we' and 'I'. Something seemed a little blurred somewhere.

'We're fine,' said Tom Keck. 'Thank you.'

'Can you still get drugs on the mainland?' asked Barbara Pulmow.

'Drugs?' asked the man.

'I mean medicines.'

'Oh, medicines,' said the man. He smiled his smile again. 'You can get most things if you can pay.'

'We don't have any money,' said Barbara. 'Do we?' she asked Pearl.

Pearl shook her head.

'Money's no good now,' said the man.

'So how can you get the drugs?' asked Barbara.

'Well, you can trade,' said the man. 'Food, for instance.'

'Oh, we've got lots of food,' said Barbara.

Henry Keck frowned. 'Not that much,' she said. 'We have to make it last.'

'Oh, yes,' said Barbara.

'Well, I'm glad to hear you've got food,' the man said. 'That's good. I'll be honest with you.'

'Yes, please,' said Pearl.

The man looked at her. 'You asked me what I want,' he said. 'Well, I'll tell you. We thought you might have some stores here. We didn't know if you'd still be alive. If there's no one alive, it's no harm to take it. I have a wife and child.'

Pearl interlaced her fingers. She put them to her chin. 'You have a wife and child?'

'Yes,' said the man.

'All right. We can let you have some food. But there will be conditions.'

The man put his hands on his hips and nodded sagely. 'I see.'

'Firstly,' said Pearl, 'you must never come back here.'

'Never come back,' echoed the man.

'Secondly, you must never tell anyone where you got the food from.'

The man nodded again. The words seemed to make sense to him. 'That it?' he asked.

'Yes,' said Pearl. 'Now I would ask you to wait here by your boat. We'll find you something, you can eat and drink and rest, and then I want you to go back before it gets dark.'

The man looked at her seriously. 'That's thirteen or fourteen miles,' he said. 'I'll never make it.'

'Those are the conditions,' said Pearl. 'There are other islands around here, as I'm sure you know. There's Mancoe, and Wideopen, and Sonnet. You can stay there.'

The man took two strides forward and grabbed Alice Celia Swash, who wanted to start her own business supplying dental products. She screamed. With his other hand he took a knife from his back pocket. None of us had seen it.

Alice bit his wrist.

The man punched Alice in the face with the knuckles of his knife-hand and Alice's nose ran blood. 'Don't bite, bitch!' he roared. He pulled her into himself. 'Now, I want food, and I want to see what you've got. Take me to the school. Or I'll hurt her. Up you go.'

'Don't let him, don't let him!' Rowena Northcote-Heathcote pleaded to no one in particular.

'We can't do anything,' hissed Amber Wells. 'He's got a knife.'

Thus a strange procession began, bound for the school, some of us ahead, some behind, the man in the centre pulling Alice, who moaned a little but was otherwise silent.

We got to the school wall and the man looked around. 'Where are the teachers?' he asked.

'There aren't any,' said Lettice Fine.

'Don't say that!' cried Hillary Kaplan.

The man smiled. 'Is that right? What happened? They die?'

'You're a horrible man,' Hillary blurted, on the edge of tears.

'These are horrible times,' the man said.

The procession reached the main door of the Shute Building. The knife was still at Alice's throat. The whole front of her blouse was stained with blood.

'Open the door,' the man said.

The procession went into the main reception lobby, with its portrait of the founder, Tabitha Shute.

Pearl stepped in front of him. 'I told you we'd give you food,' she said. 'There's no need for all this.'

The man gave his ghastly grin. In the dimmer light, his face was gaunt. 'What you said, little girl, was that you wanted me to take myself off. Well, I like it here.'

Pearl appeared to consider. 'All right,' she said. 'You can stay here. There's no need for violence. There's enough for everyone. We've got a room for you. You can rest. We can bring you something to eat in your room. Then we can bring as much food as you need for your wife and child. Of course, they'll be getting hungry.'

The man laughed a high, hysterical laugh that went on for a long time. It was easily the most frightening thing he'd done so far.

He wiped his mouth with his knife-hand. 'Where's the room?' he asked.

'Just up here,' said Pearl. She gestured towards the other girls. 'There's no need for this lot to come, is there? Go on, get back, you lot. And there's no need for Alice to be involved, now we've reached an understanding.'

'She goes with me,' said the man, still holding the knife at her throat, 'Alice does.'

'All right,' said Pearl brightly. 'I can see you need some security. But I'd like your promise you won't harm her.'

Alice let out a whining scream and struggled to get free. 'No!'

The knife barely missed slicing into her.

'Keep still!' The man bellowed. 'I'll cut you!' He held her tightly against him, her blonde hair on his half-exposed chest. 'No promises! Now, I'm tired. Where's the room?'

'Of course,' said Pearl. 'It's this way.'

Pearl led the way through the hall and into the main corridor. The rest of us hung back.

'What can we do?' whispered Lisa Plast.

'There's only one of him and there are dozens of us,' said Melissa Verne.

Pearl opened the door to Study Room F12 and ushered the man in.

Alice screamed again, this time desperate. 'Pe-e-a-arll!'

But Pearl didn't seem to hear her. 'Here you go,' she said to the man. 'Please make yourself comfortable. He won't hurt you, Alice. He's just tired after his journey. When he's got what he wants he'll go.'

'No! Please! Pe-e-a-a-arlll!'

'You'll be fine. We'll wait outside.'

The beast and Alice went into Study Room F12 and the door closed behind them. There was a click. And then silence. The study rooms were very well soundproofed.

We waited for a few seconds.

'What are you doing?' whispered Laura Huxley to Pearl.

'I don't know,' said Pearl. 'We've got to play for time.'

'He'll rape her.'

'Yes,' said Pearl. 'Yes, he might.'

Laura looked at Pearl, thunderstruck. 'What do you mean, he might? Are you out of your mind? That's illegal!'

'Yes, I'm aware it's illegal,' said Pearl.

'What do you mean play for time?'

'I have to think,' said Pearl. 'We need a weapon.'

'There's no time!' whispered Laura at gale force. 'We have to do something now.'

'Look, there's a hammer,' said Kay Hawkins. And indeed there was. Someone had been doing some repairs and there were various tools left under the sill of a window: a hammer, a saw, some sandpaper and some screwdrivers.

Kay ran to get the hammer and ran back. 'Here you are,' she said, handing it to Pearl.

Laura snatched the hammer from Pearl's grasp, and then, to my surprise, thrust it at me. I took it unwillingly and examined it. It was the type of hammer that had no claw, only a hemispherical metal bulb on one end. It had a pinewood shaft – either pine or an allied wood – and was varnished. It was stamped with the maker's name: Eliot. It felt rather light.

'Do something!' commanded Laura Huxley. 'He's in there with a knife. He might kill her.'

'He just wants food,' I managed lamely.

'He wants more than food,' seethed Laura. 'He wants her!'

'We don't know that,' I said.

'Of course he does, you eunuch!' said Laura.

'What do you want me to do?' I asked.

'I don't know, do something!'

'All right, I will,' I said with an indignation that might have been appropriate in entirely different circumstances. Holding the hammer, I strode towards the door. There was not a single thought in my head. I rapped sharply on it with the hammer. 'Excuse me,' I said.

And it was at that moment that a terrific howl of anguish erupted from behind the portal of Study Room F12. But it wasn't Alice's voice. The door opened and Alice flew out, passed us, and rushed into the driveway, making a blubbering noise.

We hurried into Study Room F12.

There on the floor was the man, on his knees, looking up at us with an expression of torment. His trousers were around his ankles. His hands were at his groin, and there was blood on his hands. The knife lay on the floor nearby. There was no blood on the knife.

'Aaaahhh!' the man moaned.

Mary-Dot Golding kicked the knife further away. I stood over the beast-man with the hammer – which I think was actually a hammer for tacks – above my head. The beast-man seemed incapable of resistance, such was his agony. He stared up at me, rocking a little backwards and forwards, his face writhing. Perhaps in that moment he wanted me to hit him.

'Get a rope,' said Pearl to Bettina Farque. 'And get me that knife.'

Bettina flew out of the door. Mary-Dot retrieved the knife. The beast-man did nothing. I continued holding the hammer over his head.

'If he moves, Stephen, hit him hard,' said Pearl.

The beast-man's head sagged, and he moaned. A semicircle of blood was expanding into the carpet. He had received some terrible injury down there. Whether it was definitely off or not was hard to say. Pearl held the knife-blade in his face. 'You brought this on yourself,' she said. 'And now a price must be paid.'

Personally I wondered whether a price hadn't already been paid. I hoped I wouldn't have to use the hammer.

Bettina returned with a rope and Zillah Smith.

'Is this him?' Zillah cried, completely unnecessarily.

'Bind him,' Pearl said.

Zillah and Mary-Dot Golding forced the man's hands behind his back. But as they attempted to tie them, the beast-man gave a cry, wrested his hands away from them and lunged at Pearl. She darted back and feinted at his fingers. The blade flicked open a flap of skin on his hand.

'Hit him!' screamed Bettina.

Trembling, I brought the hammer down as hard as I could on his head. There was a sharp crack. I recalled hitting a coconut I had won at a fair. The consonance between the two sensations was revolting.

The man fell forward. He quivered a little and lay still.

'Do his hands!' shouted Pearl.

They did them.

'Now out with him!' said Pearl. 'We'll put him in the stable. Tie a rope under his arms and drag him. We'll need about ten girls.'

Zillah, Mary-Dot and Bettina, breathing stertorously, tied a long rope under the man's arms. Then, together with Lisa Plast, Pamela Gowler, Robyn Loss-Stevenson, Jules Cashford, Sam Keller, Anne Baring and myself, dragged him out of Study Room F12. As he moved, slug-like, across the floor, he left behind a slick of blood.

'This rope has a breaking strain of two metric tonnes,' said Robyn.

'Good,' said Pearl. 'Perfect. Get him out into reception. Right, now, turn him over.'

Zillah and I lifted one side of the man's inert body and flopped him over. His injury was now plain to see. Severance was not total. The wound wept clots of purple blood.

'Pull up his trousers,' commanded Pearl.

Zillah and I did so.

'Do them up.'

The man stirred.

'Right,' said Pearl when we had finished. 'Now drag him to the stable. We want him near Murray Mint. Down the steps. Don't mind his head, he can't feel anything.'

The man's eyes, open, rolled horribly in their sockets. We jerked him forward, down the steps and into the driveway. 'Pull!' shouted Pearl. 'Pull! Pull!'

We reached the stable. Dragging him to a pillar, we positioned him sitting upright. We untied his hands, then re-tied them behind the pillar. Additional ropes secured his belly and neck. He was still only semi-conscious.

'Won't he choke?' asked Amber Wells.

'We'll loosen it later,' said Pearl.

We stood back to inspect our handiwork. He was trussed, ensanguined and unconscious. There was a violet welt on his skull where I had hit him, and blood was dribbling down his cheek.

Only Laura Huxley seemed less than satisfied. 'You were going to let him rape her,' she said to Pearl finally.

Pearl gazed into space. 'Yes, I was,' she said.

The debate on the future of the beast-man took place in the assembly hall the following day. It was now eight weeks since the end of the world.

The resolution was: 'This house believes we should execute the beast-man.' Robyn Loss-Stevenson proposed it, with Alana March seconding. Amber Wells opposed it, with Alex Featherstonehaugh seconding.

I found the name 'beast-man' a little prejudicial to a fair trial.

Robyn opened the debate. 'Rape is a capital crime in many countries. For example, Ghana.'

I had no reason to disbelieve her.

'Capital means we can execute him,' she continued.

There were murmurs of comprehension.

'Rape isn't a capital crime under the law of the United Kingdom,' she said. 'But we have the right to declare martial law. That's law in time of war. There has just been a nuclear war and there will be a lot more wars after this. Albert Einstein discovered E=mc2. He said that after the third world war the next war would be fought with bows and arrows.'

She consulted her notes, holding them close to her face. Her way of speaking was similar to Alison Barclay-Coutts's way of writing poetry.

'This man is a complete and obvious liar. He is a rapist. He threatened all of us with injury or death. If we keep him alive we'll have to feed him, and that means taking food away from us. A man can eat about 3000 calories a day and a girl about half that amount. So he'll be depriving two girls a day of food.'

'Point of information,' said Mickey Kodiak.

'Not granted,' said Duenna Gee in the chair.

'So far they've left us alone,' said Robyn. 'But there may be more like him. We'd better get used to defending ourselves. Clausewitz was a military writer of the 19th century. He said that the best form of defence is attack. That means we can defend ourselves by attacking him.'

Factual, certainly, though possibly not very logical. Robyn sat down and Amber Wells stood up for her rebuttal.

Amber Wells, I had often thought, had an archiepiscopal air about her. She was serious, discriminating, sensitive, and the last person you would ask for advice on executing anyone, unless it were a crucifixion.

'I would like to begin by pointing out,' she said, 'that his name is Fisher. He's not a beast-man. He's a man. We don't know what made him do what he did.'

'Point of information,' said Kat Egg, making the customary gesture.

'Granted,' said Duenna Gee.

'Has he had medical treatment? We should give him medical treatment under the Geneva Convention while we are deciding whether or not to execute him.'

There was silence as the girls imagined stitching up the man's wound.

'That,' Duenna Gee said finally, 'would require a separate resolution.'

Everyone seemed happy with this.

'This is a debate, not a trial,' Amber continued. 'If you want to execute someone you need a proper trial. This isn't a trial. All right, he attempted rape, but he didn't actually rape her, did he? How are you proposing to kill him, anyway? Hang him? It's ridiculous. We have to set an example to humanity. We have to show we are better than he is. Maybe we'll live to get as old as he is. Maybe one day we'll have children. When we do, we should be able to look back and say we did the right thing. To tell our children what we did.'

No one even looked at me at this juncture, and since I was the only person on the island with whom they could conceivably have children – apart from the beast-man, who was in poor condition to do any fathering – I found it a little insulting. I was, after all, the only boy *in the entire school.*

I think those words merit italics.

'Also, revenge breeds revenge,' Amber continued. 'He's got a family. If they find out we did this, they could come after us and kill us.'

Noises of support. And indeed, the practical note: how were we going to do it? Apart from hanging, there weren't too many options. We could, I supposed, drown him. Sea water would sting, though.

Alana March stood up to second. Alana, who enjoyed exams, was still upset about the death of her family in Nottingham. She turned to Amber.

'You haven't realised what's happened, have you?' she said. 'This isn't the United Nations. There's just us and these wild beasts, and there's going to be more of them. Soon, if we survive, we're going to have to get used to killing dozens of them. They're going to come over here in boats and we're going to have to kill them with bows and arrows or something before they even get here. We're going to get so used to it that we'll be saying "Oh, I killed a man this morning" and the other person will say, "Oh really, that's nice, well I killed three yesterday." Don't you see? We've got to kill him. If we keep him he'll just cost us food. And as soon as he's strong enough to get free he'll want to kill one of us. And I agree you can't kill someone without a trial but this is the trial. We haven't got time for a long trial with lawyers because there aren't any, and anyway everyone knows the facts – he tried to rape her, and he did rape her, so there's nothing to argue about.'

'Point of information,' said Polly Findhorn.

'Granted,' said Duenna Gee.

'How do you know he raped her?'

'Because he stuck it in her mouth,' said Alana.

'But that's not rape,' said Polly Findhorn, looking seriously perplexed.

'What is it then?'

'I don't know. Mouth rape.'

'Exactly,' said Alana. 'Mouth rape. That's a kind of rape. So thank you for making my point for me.' She glared. 'Anyway, we can't just sit around saying "Oh no, we have to do the right thing as we'll see it twenty years from now". What matters is that we do the right thing now, in an emergency, which is to get rid of him, because he's a threat. And it doesn't take a genius to work out that the best way to execute him is to hang him like they did in the Wild West. Put him on the back of Murray Mint and tie a rope round his neck and then let Murray Mint walk off.'

She sat down with a thump. There was a 'hear, hear' or two. Perhaps now some of the girls were thinking that the beast-man's execution might be managed. There was no way of seeing the relevant films, since the nearest cinema had been bombed, but there was a scene in *Tintin in America* that might do.

Alexandra Featherstonehaugh took her turn to rebut. Alex was a tall, motherly, intelligent girl.

'I appreciate what Alana says,' she began, 'but the fact is that it's all supposition. We don't know who might be coming after him. We don't know what we might or might not be forced to do. It might be that the next boat that comes is full of women and children. We don't really know what's happened on the mainland, but now we've got a boat maybe we can find out. He's given us that, at least. So I say keep him tied up and don't do anything hasty. He's like Murray Mint. Once we've killed him we can't ever take it back. Rape is a crime, but then murder is also a crime. It's the most serious crime of all.'

Alexandra certainly had a point. Murder was the five-star offence. But would it be murder, or retribution?

'So far we've survived,' Alexandra continued. 'Maybe we can make this place somewhere we can live. We've even done something no one else could do. We've found water. But if we start with murder we'll be starting with something evil. It will get into everything and poison everything. So I say just keep him under lock and key, feed him, make sure he doesn't escape, and wait. If he comes round he can tell us more about what happened. We can use him for information. Maybe there are loads of survivors. Maybe there's hardly anyone. Maybe loads of people have got boats. Maybe no one's got boats. Maybe radiation is killing people. Maybe it isn't. Now we can use his boat we can get drugs for Barbara. We can ask him what we need to trade for drugs. You see what I mean? A person is always worth more alive than dead. We mustn't act out of revenge.'

'Point of information,' said someone. We turned and saw that it was Alice Celia Swash. No one had seen her at the back, in the gloom. She had found a new blouse. I imagined her importing false teeth, and saw that it was a good choice.

'Granted,' said Duenna Gee.

'I agree with the opposers,' Alice said. 'Let's keep him alive. He could be useful.'

The case for the resolution collapsed.

'Six for, thirty-eight against,' said Duenna.

'That's settled then,' said Pearl, who was sitting next to Alice. 'By your leave, Madam Chairman, we'll do what Alice says.'

Supplies were holding up fairly well. The freezers were still three-quarters full, but they wouldn't last forever. Inevitably the perishable foodstuffs, such as vegetables and fruit, had been consumed or gone bad. Cheese on toast, like civilisation, was becoming a distant memory.

'We need bird-catchers,' said Pearl.

Samara Slavens, Fritzi Pietsch from Hamm (or Fritzi Hamm from Pietsch), Henry Keck and Polly Findhorn, all from Wideopen, were asked for their report.

'Some birds would be easier to catch than others,' said Samara, giving it.

'Which ones?' asked Pearl.

'The medium-sized ones by the path,' said Samara.

'What would you need to knock them out?' asked Pearl.

'I don't know,' said Samara. 'A tennis racket?'

The thought of deliberately maiming birds was unpleasant. My best friend had been a bird. I liked to watch birds. I knew about birds. I had a seabird chart on my wall. But I was not a sentimentalist.

The next morning four girls marched down the sea-path swinging tennis rackets into the breeze. Pearl and I walked behind.

'The thing is,' I said to Pearl, 'the Arctic tern is migratory. In fact they have the longest migration in the animal kingdom. They migrate from the Arctic to the Antarctic. Can you imagine? They're only here for a few months. The ones by the path will defend their nests quite vigorously at this time of year.'

'How many are there on the Islands?' Pearl asked.

'Several thousand, I should think. They're among the commonest birds here.'

We walked a little further. The roll of the sea grew louder.

'Right,' said Pearl to the girls. 'Go off the path over that way.'

Samara, Fritzi, Henry and Polly stepped gingerly off the chalk and began to fan out into the heather. Going off the path was very much against school rules. Some terns, dotted about in the herbage, began to eye them unsympathetically. The girls continued to advance. Suddenly, with an angry flap of wings, one of the terns took to the air, heading directly for Polly Findhorn. Polly screamed and turned her back on it. The tern swooped over her head, brought itself up short, hovered momentarily, and muted onto her school cap.

'Wait till they get to you and then swing!' shouted Pearl.

Another bird rocketed out of the heather and made for Henry Keck.

'Get it, Henry!'

Henry faced the tern, russet hair flying. She waited until it was almost on top of her then struck out, catching the bird's head with the wood of her racket. It fell to the ground and lay twitching.

'Well done!' said Pearl. 'Keep going!'

Now it was Fritzi's turn (or tern). Holding her racket over her shoulder in a double-handed grip like a baseball bat, she waited for her tern (or turn) to come to her, rather than she to it. Her adversary, however, erupted unexpectedly from beneath her feet. With a whoop, Fritzi struck out, her eyes closed. The bird flew round and round her, seeking an opening for beak or claw. Fritzi whirled too, thrashing the air in panic. Suddenly there was a light tap as she hit something keratinous, and the tern lay disabled on the ground. Fritzi began pounding it with the edge of her racket.

'Good shot!' cried Pearl. 'Okay, keep going! A couple more! We've got to get them while they're here! They're migratory!'

I turned my back on Fritzi, still pounding away, and walked back up the path.

'Where are you going?' asked Pearl.

I didn't reply.

My disgust was, of course, irrational. But later, as we sat around experimental plates of Arctic tern and samphire hotpot, I realised that the terns were not likely to be racketed to extinction. They tasted foul.

Pearl pushed away her helping with suppressed annoyance. 'These won't do,' she said. 'They taste like medicine. What else have we got?'

I sighed. 'Fulmars.'

'Why them in particular?'

I pushed a book towards her.

'Summary please,' said Pearl.

'The fulmar is a useful bird,' I said. 'In the nineteenth century every person on St Kilda ate four fulmars a week. They caught around twenty thousand birds a year. Somehow the fulmars kept breeding. They never ran out. When the population were evacuated in 1930 there were more fulmars there than when they started.'

'Why were they evacuated?'

'I don't know.'

'And how many do we have?'

'A lot.'

'And they taste good?'

'I don't know, but they can't be as bad as these,' I said, indicating the tern-remains. 'The other thing is they have lots of uses. Just a minute.' I flicked to the relevant page. '"No bird is of so much use to the islanders as this: the fulmar supplies them with oil for their lamps, down for their beds, a delicacy for their tables, a balm for their wounds, and a medicine for their distempers".'

'I see.'

'The fulmar is actually a type of petrel. There are a couple of other species of petrels here too. Maybe they taste the same.'

'Let's get some and find out.'

The stable had an open front, so the beast-man was visible at all times. Murray-Mint steamed nearby. He wouldn't have been any help in foiling an escape, but it's always comforting to have a horse around. Don't you think?

The day after his capture, the beast-man was still semiconscious, his head lolling and his eyes half-closed.

Taking great care, we untied him from his post. He was not playing possum. Or any other marsupial. We laid him down and covered him with a blanket. The blood had dried all over his clothes and he gave out a bad smell.

He was now secured in the following way: each hand was tied tightly by the wrist, and a rope was run from each wrist to a post left and right. That meant he could lie on his back, but could not reach either hand with the other.

A few more days passed, and the beast-man did not get up, or talk. But by the fifth day he was sitting up and leaning on his post, his hands at his sides.

A ten-foot-diameter circle had been marked around him. Food was passed into the circle by pushing in with a stick, and hauling out with a rope. With effort, the beast-man was able to feed himself; by pulling his left hand rope taut, he could gain enough slack with his right hand to reach his mouth with a spoon. He thus had a limited amount of freedom, while being restrained. *Ein wenig frei*, in the German tongue.

Girls, all from Brownstone, under the precise direction of Robyn Loss-Stevenson, guarded him around the clock in six watches of four hours each. They followed strict instructions. 1) never talk to him; 2) always remain awake and alert; 3) never, under any circumstances, enter the circle. The feeding, and, later, bucket team was organised by Mancoe.

These little rivalries help foster the right atmosphere.

About a week after his capture, Pearl, Robyn, Amber and Mary-Dot, as captains of the four houses, sat at a table placed just outside the circle. The rest of the school gathered too, cross-legged on the lawn. The beast-man slouched sullenly.

Pearl interlaced her fingers, much as she had done ten days ago at the beach. Zephyrs played through her mousy hair. It was now the first week of July, but the sun was still nowhere in evidence. Occasionally a fat raindrop fell.

'You will be kept imprisoned here until we can find you a more suitable place to stay,' Pearl said. 'You may expect a sentence of several years, at the very least.'

'You think you can keep me here?' the man said hoarsely, tugging left and right.

'Certainly,' said Pearl. 'Not only can we keep you here, but we will, and any attempt at escape will be met with force. We have weapons.'

Cheers.

'You think I'm going to sit here for the rest of my life? You're out of your mind.'

Pearl merely raised her eyebrows. 'That description would seem to apply more accurately to you,' she said. 'You are a rapist and a thief.'

Applause.

The beast-man swore. I will not say the word here. Tender minds still exist somewhere, I hope.

Pearl turned to Robyn. 'My colleague has some questions,' she said.

Robyn referred myopically to a notepad. 'How many people are left on the mainland?' she began.

'I'm not answering your stupid questions,' the man boomed. He looked around him. 'And what are you all gawping at, anyway?'

His audience drew back a little.

'As soon as I get out of here,' the beast-man continued, 'I'm going to find the whore that did this to me –' he looked down at himself – 'and I'm going to kill her.'

He pulled left and right. The ropes held.

'You deserved it,' said Mary-Dot, standing up. 'And if you don't answer our questions you won't get food.' Her voice rose angrily. 'You're a stupid man and you should be dead for what you did. No one else would be as good to you as we have, so I suggest you shut up or we will shut you up.'

Loud cheers.

'Right,' said Pearl. 'We won't talk to you and we won't help you in any way. So this is your last chance. Answer our questions.'

The man was silent.

'How many people are left on the mainland?' Robyn asked again.

Another long silence.

Pearl rose to her feet.

'I've already told you,' the man said abruptly. 'They're all dead.'

Pearl sat down. 'All of them?' she asked.

'Most of them,' said the beast-man. 'We've run out of food. All the animals have gone. Nothing grows.'

'Do you really have a wife and child?'

'That's my business.'

'Is there any government? Are there soldiers or police?'

The beast-man shook his head.

'I have a question,' said Amber Wells. 'Is anyone trying to organise society? Are there groups? Or is it just people on their own?'

'There's people on their own and there's groups,' said the man. 'The groups are more powerful. They take what they want. The people on their own hide.'

'Are there women and children?'

'Of course. But they're weaker. They need a man to protect them.'

Suddenly the irony of his remark seemed to dawn on him. He darted a hasty glance left to right, as if hoping no one had heard. But it was too late.

'Like you?' shouted a voice.

Laughter burst over the beast-man's head. On and on it went. He pulled futilely at his ropes, then let them hang slackly.

He waited until the laughter had finished. He really didn't have much choice.

It was strange for me at that moment. A half-emasculated man, being laughed at. Bound, bloodied, helpless – but I still felt he was more of a man than I was.

'How many people are going to come here, do you think?' asked Pearl when the merriment had died down.

'I don't know,' the man said huskily. 'But they'll be here. Sooner or later. This island is less than fifteen miles away. There are boats. They know you're here.'

'Let me ask you this,' Pearl said. 'If you were us, what would you do?'

It was, somehow, a Pearlish question.

The man sat back on his post, his fists in the dirt. He took a while before answering. 'Build a bloody big wall,' he said.

And out of some strange habit, he smiled.

Perhaps I should re-investigate that previous remark. My own, I mean, that he was more of a man than I was.

Well, he was thirty, and I was fifteen. So I was exactly half the man he was.

Of course, I *had* hit him over the head. But any girl could have done the same, with that hammer. Would it have made her a man?

What did being a man entail?

Fulmars nested on the low cliffs to the north-west of the island, along with guillemots, razorbills and gulls. A fulmar is quite easily caught. On encountering a fulmar, one simply throws a towel over its head. Then one has one's way with it. If there are any intact eggs after this operation, they can be taken too. 'Over the beasts of the field shall man (girl) have dominion.'

And, as the book had promised, fulmar tasted excellent – a little like tuna. If the tuna is the chicken of the sea, then the fulmar is the tuna of the air. The chicken, of course, is the tuna of the land.

Pearl asked Bettina Farque to make an experimental fulmar-lamp, which was done by setting a rope-strand wick in a milk-jug of fulmar oil. Fulmars have an oil-sac in their interiors. The lamp burned steadily and brightly, though not without a certain odour.

It was now seven weeks since the disaster. Pearl had solved the water problem and the food problem. She had solved the invasion problem. Or rather, Alice-Celia Swash had. The beast-man was restrained. Pearl was top in all subjects. Except sports.

In recognition of her services, Pearl had been appointed Head Girl, in place of Yolanda Vane-Hovell-Vane. She had also been given rooms in the Lodge, with carpets, oak bookcases and patterned armchairs. Three times a week she held an evening meal for her house captains and the occasional guest or two.

And so it was that in early July a gathering took place. It consisted of Pearl, Robyn, Mary-Dot, Amber, Tom Keck, Henry Keck, Helen Maitland (nudist parents) and myself. We were all fifteen years old, except Tom and Henry Keck, who would be fifteen in a week.

When the protected avian fauna had been consumed, and the girls were pushing back their chairs with satisfied expressions, Pearl addressed us *en bloc*. As she spoke, I began to see why she had invited me.

'I want to talk about our future,' she began. 'Here on Near. Soon we won't have any electricity. No diesel. We may as well stop using the generator as soon as the freezers are empty. We need to get used to it. We'll keep it for emergencies only. No food except what we can find or grow here. No clothes except what we can make. How long do you think we can hold out? A year? Two years? Five years?'

'In five years we'll be twenty,' said Mary-Dot vaguely.

We took a moment to imagine being twenty and dressed in feathers.

'We'll have to become the most careful people in history,' Pearl continued. 'Our lives will depend on what we can save and store up, and what we can invent. We'll have to recycle everything. We'll have to become not just the most careful people but the cleverest people.'

'What do you mean, recycle?' asked Tom Keck.

'Using things more than once,' Helen Maitland said. 'When you've finished with something, don't throw it away.'

'Oh,' said Tom.

'We'll have to take care of one another,' continued Pearl. 'Whether we live or die is up to us.'

It was an inspirational vision, in a sense. But Pearl looked glum.

'There's only one problem,' she said. 'And it comes from over there.' She pointed towards the mainland. 'The beast-man. He came to take what he wanted. He wanted our food, he wanted our supplies. And he wanted Alice. That is a reality. Unless we can defend ourselves, we won't last five minutes, let alone five years.'

'We did defend ourselves,' said Mary-Dot.

'Yes, but we were lucky,' said Pearl. 'Next time there may be more of them, or they won't be so foolish. It was a warning. A rehearsal.'

'What can we do, then?' asked Amber Wells.

'The beast-man said it. Build a wall. Make weapons. Without defences, we're easy pickings. He's done us a favour.' She paused. 'You see, men are different from women.'

Pearl turned to me. Her drooping nose was lit unflatteringly by the quavering flames of the fulmar-lamp. 'I'm sorry, Stephen. This is a reality we have to face up to. There have been great men, good men. And it is more difficult to be good than great. But what men share is the capacity to do violence to get what they want. They fight one another for prestige and power and women. That is what history is. History is men.'

Henry Keck laughed. Perhaps she was thinking of me. Pearl, however, quelled her with a look.

'Don't be under any illusion. When the male nature – the warrior nature – is allowed to prevail, women and children suffer.'

'But if we make weapons,' asked Amber, 'aren't we just as bad as them?'

'No,' Pearl said. 'No. The rapist is not the same as the girl who defends herself.'

'Aren't Christians pacifists?' persisted Amber.

Pearl said nothing.

'Are you still a Christian?'

'There's more than one way of being a Christian,' Pearl said after a while. 'One way is to defend yourself from evil. Defend the school.'

'I'm not violent,' I blurted out. It was mortifying, really.

'I know you're not,' said Pearl. 'But I'm not talking about you, as a person. Although, even you, I can see…' She paused, smiling faintly. 'Well, I shouldn't say anything about you. You're working hard for the school.'

'What I don't see,' said Mary-Dot, 'is how we can build a wall round the whole school.'

'Haven't we already got a wall?' asked Amber.

'That's no good,' said Pearl. 'That wouldn't keep a flea out. I'm talking about a proper wall. Twenty feet high.'

'Twenty feet – that's six and two thirds yards,' said Robyn.

'That's right,' said Pearl. 'Exactly. Right round the school. Only not as long as the wall is at the moment. To go all round would take too much timber. I'm thinking of a wall that would enclose the main buildings, the dormitories and the Lodge. And the well. I'll show you.'

She took a piece of paper and sketched out a plan of the school, plus a wall. It was about half of the length of the current school boundary. Outside, she sketched furious crosses. These were, I supposed, *men*.

'It wouldn't include the chapel, the tennis courts, the outbuildings, the sports block or the vegetable garden,' she said. 'But it'd have everything inside it we'd need if there were a siege.'

'A siege?' asked Amber.

'They want to get in. We want to keep them out,' said Pearl. 'A siege.'

'Wouldn't we need the vegetable garden?' asked Henry.

'We'll need it in normal times, yes,' said Pearl. 'We just won't defend it. We'll have plenty of provisions inside the walls. We'll wait them out. That's what a siege is. It's a waiting game. It's a game of psychology.'

'Where did you get all this?' asked Amber.

'There's a book I've been reading,' Pearl said.

'What?'

'Julius Caesar,' said Pearl. 'The Romans put up a ten-mile wall around a hilltop. In just a couple of weeks. We can do the same.' She referred to her map. 'Except in our case, the wall has to be a third of a mile. Five hundred yards. We'll need to cut down a lot of trees. Dig ditches.'

'How can we lift trees?'

'Murray Mint will help us. We have the tools, we have the womanpower, and the horsepower. It's literally either that, or we accept that we are going to be invaded.'

There was a long silence.

'In fact,' said Pearl, standing up and clearing away some of the plates, 'I don't think we really have a choice.'

As soon as Pearl said that we had no choice, I knew that such a wall was, in a sort of way, already a reality.

Es muss sein. It must be. Did her self-assurance derive from her Germanic heritage? She was Pearl Wyss, after all.

My heritage was on the Spanish side of things. We are more Catholic and mystical. We have a taste for saints and angels. There is no room for an *es muss sein* if there is not also an *es muss nicht sein.*

Of course, I didn't believe in any such saints. But neither did I have my own personal *es muss sein.*

'Titty, you will be mine.' That was not a thought I had ever entertained. 'One day I will import dental products.' Ditto. 'We have no other choice.' Ditto. I took after neither my mother nor my father, each strong in their own way.

It takes strength to desert one's son and heir, I imagine.

Readers will remember that one of the unexpected benefits of having your island raided by a famished rapist is that he may arrive in a boat, which, when he is imprisoned and immobilised via a wound to his privy member, may devolve to his captors.

With this truth in mind, Pearl decided that it would be a good idea to make a journey to Wideopen. Wideopen was a small island about a mile to the east, and thus perhaps within our navigational capabilities. Seals lived there in huge numbers. In fact, they lived there and nowhere else. Not a single seal had ever been spotted on Near. Seals are fastidious like that.

The expedition members would be myself, Karen Dworkin, Zillah Smith and Bee Wasket.

Karen Dworkin was a whiz with racket, bat, club and stick. She was thus quite sturdily built. So were Bee and Zillah. We four were the beefiest the school could provide. In truth, I was the least beefy of the party, but perhaps Pearl felt that she had better start developing my potential.

We picked a morning when the sea was calm, and took a few practice rides back and forth in the bay. They seemed to go well enough. The beast-man had rowed himself the thirteen miles to Near with an oar in each bearded hand; we took it in turns to sit side by side in the middle of the boat, pulling one oar each. The arrangement suited us, since one pair could relieve the other; but with four sailors on board, progress was ponderous. Nevertheless, at about ten o'clock, we thought it time to strike out for Wideopen, clearly visible across the sound. After some encouraging words from Pearl, we waved goodbye to Near and made for the seal-grounds.

I will confess that I had severe misgivings about the whole thing. We could see Wideopen quite plainly – we could even see the seals, black maggots infesting the beach – but we had no real idea of how long it would take us to get there. We had no notion of tides or winds, or their possible influence on our efforts.

Above, the cloud cover was total. Occasionally a low-running cloud, like a visiting beluga, drifted soundlessly over our heads.

On board, we had provisions for three days, chiefly in the form of canned food, boiled seabird eggs, and various other delicacies prepared by Elizabeth Pelham. In case we were forced to stay over on the island, we had a four-man tent with sleeping-bags. I would bunk in with the girls.

For all practical purposes, I *was* a girl.

We rowed for two hours, changing seats every half an hour or so. The wind picked up and began to whine through our clothes. During those two hours, Wideopen did not get appreciably nearer – although Near did appear to recede. We seemed not so much to be covering space as creating space. The oars rose and dipped. And then, to our dismay, it started to rain.

For some reason, no one had foreseen it might do this. We had no waterproof clothing. The rain began collecting in a little radioactive pond in the bottom of the boat.

Wideopen was still far away, and the weather had become noticeably colder. Some sort of current was dragging us off to the left of our target. However much we steered for Wideopen, the boat seemed to want to bypass it.

We pulled for another couple of hours, but had now been carried so far to the left of Wideopen that both Near and Wideopen were receding behind us. It was about two o'clock, and we had been rowing for four hours.

'What are we going to do?' asked Bee.

'There's no point fighting this current,' I said, breathing heavily. 'We'll just get exhausted.'

'What brilliant advice,' said Bee. 'Let's just relax and die.'

'I'm hungry,' said Zillah.

A fulmar flapped slowly by, eyeing us speculatively.

'We can't eat now,' I said. 'We've got to think.'

'Can't we think on a full stomach?' asked Zillah.

Waves knocked lazily at the keel. To the west lay home. To the east, Wideopen. In the direction we were headed was, I estimated, Holland. All well and good, especially if you like dykes and Hollandaise sauce. Except that Holland was 400 miles away, and we were drifting at a rate of about a mile an hour. That was about two weeks at sea. We had three plastic bottles of water between us, and enough food for a couple of days. We might survive for two weeks by drinking one another's blood, but that assumed we were neither becalmed, nor taken by another current, nor capsized by a storm, nor subject to any of the other fates of ocean castaways. Holland-bound was Hades-bound.

Meanwhile, it continued to drizzle.

'Look at it this way,' I said. 'Why are we going in this direction? There's no wind. So it must be the current. The current is going in between the islands and it's pushing us out to sea.'

'So?' asked Bee.

'It's like a funnel,' I said. 'The current is squeezed through the funnel and it comes out the other side. Then it spreads out. We're in the spread-out part.'

'How do you know that?'

'Well, actually, I don't,' I admitted. 'I'm just hoping we are.'

'I don't get it,' said Zillah. 'What are you talking about?'

Karen gazed, lost, at the misty horizon. 'It will be getting dark in a couple of hours,' she said.

Zillah's face registered panic: staring eyes and laboured breathing. She stumbled forward to grab the oars from me. 'We've got to row!' she said. 'There's no point in talking!'

'Just a minute!' I cried. 'Please! Let me finish! It depends how far we are from the edge of the stream. The funnel. If we can just get to the other side of this funnel we might be able to double back and approach Wideopen from the far side.'

'Wow, did you see that?' asked Karen, still staring horizon-wards.

We looked where she had pointed. Soon, about a hundred yards away, a black back broke the water. Seals. Lots of them. And they were all heading for Wideopen.

'We'd be all right if we could swim like that,' said Bee.

'Why are they there, though?' I asked excitedly. 'They're over there for a reason! They're not here, are they?'

'No, they'd be in a boat,' said Zillah.

'I mean, they're going with the current!' I said. 'Can't you see? That must be where the edge is! If we can get over there we can follow them!' I stood up and shouted. 'Follow the seals! Follow the seals!'

'He's gone crazy,' said Karen.

'It's hunger,' said Zillah.

I sat back down again. 'Listen. Just humour me. Make for where the seals are and I promise you we can get to Wideopen. Just a little bit more. We just have to cut across this current and we'll be free.'

Bee regarded me sceptically. 'All right,' she said at length. 'One more try. You and Zillah take the oars.'

Zillah and I took our positions. We pulled hard, heading for the place where we'd last seen the seals. And then suddenly the sideways motion of our boat seemed to slacken off. With a deliciously smooth motion, like ice-cream sliding down a mirror, a current caught us – the one that the seals had been following – and we were carried directly for Wideopen.

'Hurrah!' cried Zillah. 'Seals for dinner!'

Rowing was easy now. With each stroke, Wideopen loomed larger before us. In another hour we were at the far side of the island, out of sight of the school.

We beached the boat, staggered onto the strand and flung ourselves down on it. Cannibalism on the open sea was not, for the moment, on the agenda.

For ten minutes we did nothing but lie on the ground and groan. It was still drizzling, but the rain felt kind. It was terrestrial rain. Eventually we picked ourselves up, stumbled to the boat and retrieved the tent and supplies. We pitched the aforementioned on a dune above the tide line, and bundled inside. We took off our wet outer clothing, hung it from the apex of the tent and got into our sleeping bags. I think we had largely forgotten that we were there to kill a seal. I suppose it was now about four o'clock, and getting dark.

Someone was shining a torch in my face.

'Oh, he's awake,' said Bee.

The other two girls were also awake, eating nuts in honey.

'We're having a midnight feast,' said Karen. 'Do you want some?'

'What's the time?' I asked.

Bee checked her watch. 'Two o'clock in the morning,' she said.

'Okay.'

'Give him some nuts,' ordered Bee.

'Here you go,' Karen said, laughing as she tossed over the jar.

I ate for a time in the steamy tent, propped up on one elbow. There was a smell of damp vinyl. Bee set the torch aside so it cast a low light on the floor. She stretched out on her back. Her sleeping bag had slipped down to her waist.

'Stephen,' she said. 'I'm cold.'

'Do your sleeping bag up, then.'

'Can't you lie next to me?' she said sweetly.

'I *am* lying next to you.'

'Come closer.' Her tone changed. 'Now.'

I put the jar aside and wormed my way over to her. The two other girls stifled giggles.

'That's not good enough. In fact it's rubbish. You're not a very good lover.'

'I didn't say I was,' I said uneasily.

'Get out of your sleeping bag, you numbskull, and lay on top of me, so you really warm me up. Come on, I won't hurt you.' She grabbed my arm. 'Do it!' she commanded.

I got out of my sleeping bag and lay on her body. The school had once owned a spacehopper. Occasionally I would lie on it face down, rolling idly backwards and forwards, testing my own weight. Lying on Bee was like that. I thought I must be heavy. But Bee didn't seem to mind.

She put her arms round me. 'Take your shirt off,' she said.

'Why?' I asked.

'Just do it.'

Still on top of her, and with difficulty, I pulled my school shirt over my head.

'Wow, you're so thin!' said Bee.

'He's like a lacrosse stick,' said Karen. 'With a head instead of a net.'

'Yes, but he's got some muscles,' said Bee. 'Look.'

Zillah snorted. 'He needs to do push-ups.'

'Go on, Stephen,' said Karen. 'Do push-ups.'

'What was it like when you hit the beast-man?' Bee asked me.

'I don't know,' I said.

'You gave him a whack.'

I couldn't think of anything to say. The memory was still painful.

'How do you feel now?' asked Bee. 'Is it nice?'

And in fact it was nice, to be eating nuts and honey, after having just escaped death by drowning, and lying on top of a girl, even if you were afraid she'd get you in a headlock at any moment. I suppose male praying mantises feel the same way.

'Yes, it's nice,' I said. And kissed her.

'Right! Get him off me!' cried Bee. She pushed me off in a single movement. 'Come and help me!' she shouted to Zillah and Karen.

The two girls knee-shuffled towards me with determined expressions.

'Let me see!' Bee said to me.

'See what?' I replied.

'Let me see it.'

I backed away as far as I could.

'Get him,' said Bee.

The other two girls seized me with blistered hands. I struggled. They were stronger than me, but I had my honour to protect. I elbowed Zillah in the jaw. She retired. After much struggling, my fist connected with Karen's nose and she overbalanced and landed with a thump in the corner. Only Bee was left. We crouched, facing one another in deadly earnest, breathing heavily in a nest of twisted sleeping bags.

'That's enough,' I shouted, humiliated down to my socks. 'If anyone else touches me I'm calling the police.'

The remark caused hysteria.

'All right, Stephen, I'm sorry,' said Bee, still laughing. 'We shouldn't have done it. If you want to kiss me, you can.'

'Go jump in the lake,' I said. I got into my sleeping bag, zipped it up and scowled at them.

Bee reached out slowly and stroked my hair. I threw her hand off. Then, with a lunge, she planted a kiss on my cheek. 'Sorry,' she said. She turned off the torch. 'Come on, let's get some sleep.'

The kiss lingered on my skin for some time. After a while, I heard snores. Then I drifted off to sleep, dreaming of Titty.

The best way to kill a seal is really the same as the best way to kill anything else. You simply walk up to it and hit it on the head with a hammer.

On Wideopen, at the far side of the island, there was an enormous herd of them, just lying on the gravel. A group of animals less affected by a nuclear war it was difficult to imagine. They didn't even seem singed.

The very first seal we approached, which I think was a young female, gave us a look like a hotel receptionist greeting a valued customer.

'Who's going to do it?' asked Bee.

No one said anything.

'Give me the hammer,' Bee said.

Zillah handed it to her. Bee brought the hammer down on the seal's skull. It collapsed, stone dead.

Karen went over to examine it. She tried to lift it. 'This one's too heavy,' she said. 'It weighs a ton.'

'What's the point of coming all the way here for a small one?' asked Bee.

'It'll sink the boat,' said Karen.

'No it won't,' said Bee. 'I'm not doing another one just for you. Stephen, give her a hand.'

We manhandled the seal into the boat. The other seals didn't seem to object to the procedure. We packed up the tent.

Now it was time to negotiate the channel and return to Near.

'What we need to do,' I said, 'is to make for a point a long way to the right-hand side of the island. And then, when the current catches us, it will wash us directly home. That way, we use the current to our advantage.'

'All right,' said Bee.

The seal, dead in the bottom of the boat, did not have an opinion. I hoped it was not the seal that had shown us the way to Wideopen.

It was a dry day with little wind. We pushed off and rounded the island. We could now see Near clear in the near-distance. We rowed for an hour to get a good way from the tip of Wideopen before changing course and heading into the current. However, just as the current started to catch us, a disaster occurred. During a changeover of oarsmen, as we stumbled with drunken legs about the boat, an oar fell over the side. Before we could grab it, it was floating away from us. Short of diving in, there was no way we could reach it. Oar and boat diverged like disappointed lovers.

'You idiot!' screamed Bee at Zillah, who was nearest the offense. 'Quickly!'

Frenziedly I tried to paddle with the single remaining oar, but the exercise was futile. One oar just turned us in a circle, and while we were changing sides, the other oar got further away. Eventually, all could do was watch it drift off. We had lost the implement that would have enabled us to row to retrieve the implement that would have enabled us to row.

It seemed, on the face of it, fatal. We had one oar and a mile to go.

But that was not to reckon with the force of the current. The bow of the boat was now facing Near, and Near was our destination. All we needed to do was move across the channel as the current took us inexorably with it. And we found, to our joy, that by rowing mainly on the Near side, with a few corrections on the Wideopen side, we were able to move ourselves slowly in the required direction. The current did all the work. After two hours, we were beaching ourselves on

Near, seal and all, and a welcoming committee was running to throw its arms around us.

Seeing Titty among the girls, I hauled the seal from the bottom of the boat and dumped it onto the sand in front of her.

'You got a sea-lion,' said Titty.

'It's a seal,' said Karen.

'Are you sure it's dead?' asked Lisa Plast.

'Seals are warm-blooded,' I said. 'Feel it. It's cold.'

Lisa bent down. 'No it's not,' she said.

I felt the seal's hide. She was right. 'Well, seals have a lot of stored-up warmth,' I said. 'It will take a while to…'

And it was at that moment that the seal opened its eyes. It looked like a hotel receptionist who is now regrettably forced to charge extra for breakages.

'It's alive!' shrieked Zillah.

Everyone stepped back guiltily. The seal got up onto its flippers and explored the air with its nose. Then it began to lumber down the beach.

'Get it!' screamed Bee.

But it was too late. The seal was already at the water's edge. It gave a couple of sharp flipper-thrusts, slipped into the water and was gone.

'Well, at least we know we can do it,' Pearl said later. 'And we can always make another oar. We have plenty to eat for now and I'm sure someone can hit the seal a bit harder next time. That was quite a success, in fact. You've found out something very useful. Currents are treacherous around here. Rowing isn't as easy as it looks. But next time we'll be prepared. We'll get all the seals we want. Well done, everyone.'

The beast-man, who now had a thicker beard, had been confined in the stable for a fortnight. But our method of restraining him could not be employed forever. We needed to move him to a more practical location.

This was done in the following way.

First, a cage was constructed by Bettina Farque. Eleven feet long and seven feet wide, it was made from thick spars of wood bolted tightly at the interstices, the nuts securely countersunk. It had a flat wooden roof at the top, tilted at a slight angle to let the water run off, and a barred door with a lock. Inside was a plain pallet-bed with a mattress taken from the Lodge. The cage was situated in the open air, as before, near the entrance to the Shute Building, so that we could observe the beast-man at all times: and, as before, a ten-foot circle was inscribed around it.

The only problem was how to get the beast-man from his current accommodations into the cage.

Pearl's plan involved the use of Murray Mint. First, the beast-man's left-hand rope was attached to Murray Mint's collar. Of course, this was the most dangerous point of the procedure, since the beast-man could have attempted to break free in the interval between untying the rope from the pillar and attaching it to Murray Mint. In order to preclude this, a second rope was secured to the first at a point just before it reached the pillar, using a knot found in *The Puffin Book of Knots*. This rope was then run to Murray Mint, and attached to him before severing the connection to the pillar. Helen Maitland, whose parents were nudists, walked Murray Mint forward to keep up the rope tension. A similar knot was then attached to the right-hand rope and held by twelve of the strongest girls, with Paula Ott, the fattest girl in the year, at the end, the rope wrapped around her waist. This rope's connection to the right-hand pillar was then severed, and Murray Mint was given the command to walk on. The procession of one horse, one beast-man and twelve girls then made its way the short distance to the cage.

On reaching the door to the beast-man's new residence, Murray Mint was halted, and a rope taken off the collar line, threaded through the cage door, across the breadth of the cage, out the side and twice around a tree a few yards away. This rope was then held secure by a further group of girls (and myself). All that remained was for the rope to the collar to be cut and for the twelve girls (and myself) to take up the slack and draw the beast-man into the cage. When we had drawn him as far as possible across its breadth – until his arm, with the rope tied to it, was sticking out of the bars on the far side – we severed the rope held by Zillah's girls, and closed and locked the door. Finally, the tree-tensioned rope could be cut. The beast-man could now take up residence. Both his wrists were still bound, but he had both hands free, and could thus assist himself in undoing the ropes, which had about six feet of slack on each hand.

This operation was conducted in silence. I mean that no one addressed the beast-man. If the beast-man spoke, no one responded. There were however plenty of exhortatory cries from one girl to another as they pulled the ropes, cut them, secured them, and so on. I think that the beast-man had become so accustomed in the previous two weeks to never receiving a reply, that he had stopped making much attempt at speech. During the first days of his imprisonment he had made ribald, angry, pleading, mocking or philosophical remarks to anyone within range, trying elicit a response, if only a smile or a nod; but lately he had given up.

There was only one point at which he did speak. This was after the cage door had been shut and locked and he was looking round at his new home for the first time. He brought his hands together, rubbed them, examined his wrists, and gazed out at us.

'Murray Mints, Murray Mints, too good to hurry mints,' he sang.

It was about three months since I had last watched television.

The debate on the fortification of the school took place on Tuesday the 29th of July, 1975. It was now just over three months since the end of the world.

The resolution was: 'This house believes that the school should be protected by a twenty-foot high, five-hundred-yard long wall.'

Proposing the resolution was Pearl herself, seconded by Francesca Mond. Opposing the resolution was Laura Huxley, seconded by myself. Yes, me.

We hadn't had much of a summer. The hall felt damp. Cold sea-draughts blew through cracks in windows and doors; lights were off for most of the evening, and not on at all during the day; sand and dirt had collected in the corridors. May Sussums was ill and no one knew what was wrong with her. Clumps of Patsy Hugenoth's hair had fallen out; this was particularly painful for her, since she was obsessed with princesses. Why more of us had not succumbed to radiation sickness was a puzzle.

Pearl, however, was cheerful as she stood up to propose the resolution.

'I believe that we are the luckiest girls alive,' she began.

There were no howls of delighted approbation.

'Just think about it. We live on an island miles away from the mainland. Everyone over there is either dead or dying.

They've run out of food. They're killing each other over what's left. Would you really like to be over there?'

No one said anything. No one wanted to be over there. But then no one really wanted to be over here either.

'We've got loads of food and we've got a whole island full of good things to eat. We've got seabirds that can supply us with oil and eggs, as well as meat. We've got puffins and rabbits. We've got seals. We've got vegetables we can grow ourselves. And we've got water, fresh water. Pure water. Not polluted or radioactive. Water from the beginning of time. Beautiful water. This is not a horrible prison in the middle of nowhere. This is a sanctuary. It's a sort of miracle. Why it was given, we'll never know. It's just a miracle. We must look after it, tend it, respect it and be thankful for it.'

'Amen,' said someone religious.

'I want to say something about the war,' Pearl continued. 'That was not a war. That was an explosion of stupidity. That was an expression of the sickness we had allowed to fester inside us. It was caused by pride, greed, and lust for power. And it was caused by men. There weren't any women setting those things off. Men did it. And now there are no more men. Not here, anyway.'

As you can imagine, I was mightily taken aback by this. She seemed to be asserting that I, Stephen Ballantyne, her debating partner, did not actually exist. And what about the beast-man?

'So what I want to say,' Pearl went on, 'is that unless we protect ourselves from these men who have destroyed the world, they will come for us. Don't think that they'll just ignore this little paradise. They'll want it for themselves. And when they arrive here, they won't take any account of what *we* want. Unless we stop them, they'll ruin everything. We must defend ourselves. So I propose this resolution in the name of self-defence.'

Some sporadic clapping.

Pearl's opening speech having concluded, Laura Huxley stood up to oppose. Laura had a bob haircut and a cut-glass accent. You may remember that Laura had remonstrated with Pearl over her conduct on the day of beast-man's arrival. In point of fact, Laura's dislike of Pearl ran deeper. Laura was from one of the wealthiest families in England. On holidays she went home either to her family's pile in the country, or to Switzerland for skiing. Pearl, by contrast, went home to a small terraced house in North London, where her parents must have been frankly perplexed by her. Some things are hardy enough to survive even a nuclear war. Seals and class-consciousness are two of them.

'I'm sorry, but all of this sounds a bit mad,' Laura said. 'All of us have got fathers or brothers or uncles. Are they all rapists and beasts? All right, we had the beast-man, but why would we judge everyone else by him? Do you mean to say if your brother or your pa turned up outside this wall you'd keep him out? It's nonsense. We can't keep people out. We need help!'

Laura's eyes filled with ready tears. Indeed, we did need help. We were only fourteen or fifteen. Most of us had fathers. Some had pas. What wouldn't we give to have those pas here, folding us in their manly arms, reassuring us, protecting us? At least a hatful of fulmar eggs.

Instead, all we had was Pearl. And her wall.

'We need help!' Laura repeated. 'Not everyone over there is crazy. All right, there was a war, but why do you blame men for that? My mother supported nuclear bombs. I heard her saying it. I remember her watching television and saying that the people protesting about nuclear bombs needed a bath. It was women just as well as men. No one thought the bombs would go off. They knew that if the Russians had them, we had to have them too, to protect ourselves.'

The fact that this argument could still be advanced after a Europe-wide cataclysm was rather striking. Some ideas just seem to go on and on.

'So I think that the proposers of this resolution have a strange view of human nature. If we're going to survive, we're going to need to co-operate with whoever's left. Men or women. And there's another thing. If we're never allowed to meet any boys, who are we going to marry when we grow up?'

A tremor ran up the spines of the audience. Marriage. Of course. Perhaps it was still possible. And, actually, why not? There were still boys in this world, presumably. Somewhere. Were the audience to become nuns, and the island a convent?

Catching the mood of the audience, Laura turned to Pearl. 'Does Pearl want us to live for the rest of our lives on this island without getting married?' she asked.

It was a good opening speech.

Francesca Mond then stood up to second the resolution. Clever, attractive, and with an affinity for stationery, it was rumoured that Francesca had a boyfriend at home. I wondered whether this would aid her in seconding Pearl's argument, viz. that all men were evil.

She stood up holding a stylish clip-binder. 'Pearl has told you what she thinks will happen,' she said, 'and I agree with her. I think what she says will come true. Men will come here to get what they want, and what they want is food and sex.'

The professional note.

'Those on the opposing side are thinking like girls. Like females. They're not thinking like men. Females try to co-operate. Females think about getting married. Boys don't give a stuff about getting married. Their minds are only on one thing. And I'm just referring to boys here. When they grow up into men they get together into armies and they come looking for women. When the Russians went into Berlin in the Second

World War they raped every woman in sight, even young girls. Even old women. The Japanese did it to the Chinese in Nanking. They raped and killed. They went into the hospitals and they turned the women out of their beds and they raped them on the floor.' Her voice rose. 'Now the Americans are doing the same in Vietnam. For men it's what makes war fun.'

I tried to scrutinise my own deepest attitudes to the fair sex. The scrutiny turned up about as much desire to rape as desire to eat an Arctic tern.

'Do you remember what the beast-man said?' continued Francesca. 'He said: "I'll kill the whore". Do you remember that? First they want us for sex, and if we don't give it to them, we're whores.'

Rowena Northcote-Heathcote put her hand on her head. 'Point of information,' she said.

'Granted,' said Eufemia Paleocapa.

'What are whores?'

'A whore is a bad woman,' said Eufemia Paleocapa.

'Oh,' said Rowena Northcote-Heathcote.

'It's a woman who gives away sex for free,' said Francesca.

'Point of information,' said Lettice Fine.

'Granted,' said Eufemia.

'I don't understand all this stuff about sex all the time. What's that got to do with it?'

There was a pause while Francesca consulted her papers.

'All right, Lettice,' she said. 'I found this in the library. I want to read it to you. It's from a book about a tribe of Indians in Canada. "They waited until all the men and boys had left the village and then they attacked. They raped the women and girls and killed them. They mutilated their bodies. Then they stuffed fish into them."'

There was a long, long pause.

'That's disgusting,' said Laura Huxley. 'Why would they do that?'

'You are out of order,' said Eufemia to Laura.

'I don't care,' said Laura.

Francesca said nothing. She sat down.

It was my own turn to speak.

Laura had done a good job, but now Francesca had undone it. I would be the last to speak. I had to say something sensible.

I stood up. 'The average width of the trees on this island is about twelve inches,' I said.

Silence.

'I mean that Pearl's fence is supposed to be five hundred yards long. Five hundred yards divided by a foot is fifteen hundred. That's one thousand five hundred. One thousand five hundred trees. That's impossible. We can't build it. Even with a horse. It would take years. We should be prepared to defend ourselves, I agree with that. But let's spend our time making bows and arrows. Let's do shooting practice. Let's make ourselves into a proper fighting force. If we build this wall we'll have no time to do anything else. And there's no guarantee we can finish it in time anyway.'

I paused.

'Is that all?' asked Eufemia, looking at me through alluringly severe Tuscan lashes.

'No,' I said. 'Pearl thinks all men are evil. That's just not true. Men and women are the same. What about Indira Gandhi? She's the president of India, and she declared war on Pakistan. Isn't it better to talk about humans rather than men? Humans are capable of evil. Men are capable of evil. Women are capable of evil. As far as the war is concerned, if there's any fault, it's the fault of the scientists who developed the weapons. When weapons are that powerful even the smallest mistake can lead to disaster. Maybe the whole thing was an accident. Maybe it was a computer. You can't base the whole of your lives on avoiding men, keeping them out. Let's say we survive for another twenty years. How will this island survive with no men? I mean, with only me?'

Laughter.

'There's no way to keep this island going without boys. So the whole thing doesn't make any sense. That doesn't mean we shouldn't have weapons. We defeated the beast-man because of weapons. But we were lucky. If we'd had bows and arrows trained on him from the moment he set foot on the island, he wouldn't have tried to grab Alice. We need to be practical, to do what we can. But building a wall is just impractical.'

I sat down. Laura glowered at me. I supposed it was because I had made no mention of marriage.

'Okay,' said Eufemia. 'I turn it over to the two principal speakers for summary rebuttal. Pearl first.'

Pearl stood up with the patient smile of a girl convinced that she can persuade a roomful of teenage girls to spend the next few years of their lives hauling logs.

'Stephen,' she said, 'opposes the resolution because he says that it is waste of effort. He says that weapons are enough, and that we can just fight them off. As long as every girl is armed, then we should be able to resist them. That's right, isn't it, Stephen? In fact, what Stephen is proposing is a battle. Of course, it would be a battle in which we couldn't retreat, because we'd have nowhere to go.' She looked at me as if I were a specimen in a bottle. 'This is the male mind in action. You can see it here for what it is.'

The girls examined me with forensic curiosity.

'Stephen prefers the excitement of a bloodbath to the construction of sensible defences that make that bloodbath unnecessary. A clearer demonstration of the difference between men and women couldn't be imagined.'

Laughter.

'Stephen also claims that the wall is impossible. It is absolutely not impossible. It is perfectly possible. There are at least ten thousand trees on this island. There are fifty-five of us. We'll have teams on the cutting, teams on the trimming, and teams on the hauling. All the trees are within a few hundred yards of where they need to go. We have ropes. We have Murray Mint. Any large project such as this one is about the application of science, organisation and hard work. There is absolutely no reason why we couldn't do it. Also, you are wrong about the trees. The mean average width of the trees is probably about a foot, but we'll take the younger trees. They'll be easier to cut and to haul. We won't just make a wall, we'll make a perimeter walkway inside the wall, and ditches outside the wall. We'll do all this and we'll learn to shoot bows too, but not to prepare for a useless war which would get us all killed. To *prevent* a useless war which would get us all killed.

'To Laura, I would say that I certainly sympathise with her desire to get married, but I would like to get married on my own terms, not on the terms of a caveman with a spear. I would say to her that she has underestimated the consequences of a catastrophic collapse of civilisation. The airwaves are dead. There is no longer any BBC. It's clear from the evidence that there is no longer any order. There is no longer any marriage. There is no longer any respect for the rights of women or children. These rights have ceased to exist. Society has ceased to exist. Marriage is now a fantasy. We cannot afford fantasies. In summary, everything has changed. We must adapt ourselves to the new reality. The post-war reality. In this reality, the strong rule over the weak. The beast-man we should regard as a representative example of the prevailing ethos.'

I felt that with this word 'ethos', which was new to me at the time, and yet which I intuitively understood to mean 'moral atmosphere', the debate was lost.

'I say protect ourselves from him and his kind,' said Pearl. 'And the only protection is a wall.'

Applause.

Laura stood up. Pearl was right: Laura's speech had focussed almost exclusively on marriage. I couldn't remember why at the time it had appeared so persuasive.

Laura seemed to fizz with frustration. 'If you think I'm going to spend my time building this useless wall then you're out of your mind. I won't live in the world you want to live in. I want a normal life. We've got a boat. Why don't we just go, and find someone who will help us? If they won't come here, then let's go to them. This whole idea of living on this island forever – it was all right with teachers and lessons, but to live here forever is just stupid. You said my idea was a fantasy, but your idea' – she jabbed a forefinger at Pearl – 'is a worse fantasy. You want to build a castle? It's ridiculous. We could never do it. Just because you found water. Next you'll be telling us we should build airplanes out of pine trees.' She turned back to the audience. 'She's dangerous. Half of you do everything she says. Listen to me! How is the world going to continue if there isn't any marriage any more? It doesn't make sense. So I oppose the resolution and I urge you to vote against it.'

She sat down with a look of disgust.

The vote was taken.

'In favour of the resolution,' said Eufemia Paleocapa, 'Thirty-nine. Against, eleven. The resolution is carried.'

So my rebellion against Pearl came to nothing.

We'd got eleven votes. These were chiefly Laura's friends, who were all rich girls: Beulah Gaze, who hated blubber and whose father owned a helicopter in which he had conspicuously failed to come and rescue her; Pamela Gowler, who was well-connected and musical; and Paula Ott, who didn't ski, but whose family ran a business that supplied equine blood transfusions. A couple of others were perhaps momentarily captivated by the idea that the future might turn out as planned and they would meet some not-very-irradiated boy and settle down in some not-very-irradiated corner of the former Home Counties.

In the corridor outside the assembly hall, I found myself walking next to Alison Barclay-Coutts. I hadn't talked to Alison since the business with Titty. In fact, Alison had been sent to Coventry, and it was inadvisable to have much to do with her.

'I voted for you,' she said.

'Thank you,' I said softly, not really looking at her.

'I voted for you,' she continued, 'because I felt it had to be true, what you said. That you're not evil.'

'Oh,' I said.

'I don't believe you're any more evil or any more good than anyone else. Pearl obviously thinks you're evil. But you're just an average human being.'

I didn't like the insistence on my mediocrity. 'Listen, I'm sorry no one's talking to you, Alison,' I said.

'That's all right,' she said. 'Some people still talk to me. Pearl does. So does Jules.'

'Can't you make it up with Titty?'

'I've tried, but she's not interested.' She paused. 'I think you and I have a lot in common, Stephen.'

I swallowed. 'What do you mean?' I asked.

'Well, it must be lonely being the only boy in the school. We're both lonely people.'

'Oh, that,' I said.

We were now in the corridor near the classrooms. She was due to go straight on towards the dorms, and I was planning on going for a walk outside.

'I wanted to ask about Albert,' she said. 'What do you think happened to him?'

'I don't know,' I said. 'My best guess is that the door opened and he flew out, and then someone closed it.'

'Oh, I see,' she said. 'I miss him.' She walked on without saying goodbye, but then turned and looked back at me over her shoulder. 'Do you ever hear him singing?'

'No,' I said.

She shrugged and walked off.

A couple of days later, Pearl buttonholed me. She was by the Lodge talking with a group of girls: Titty, Paula Ott, Henry and Tom Keck (who, the inattentive reader may need to be reminded, were not boys), Alana March, Deedee Foe and Sam Keller.

She left the group and came over to speak to me. 'I wanted to thank you for the debate last Monday,' she said. 'We're very lucky to have you.'

'I thought you saw me more or less as an unwholesome influence,' I said.

The other girls began to drift over to us.

'Yes, but that's why I like you, Stephen,' Pearl said.

'You like unwholesome influences?'

Deedee Foe, coming up to us, laughed. Titty, who was with her, didn't laugh. I had never heard Titty laugh.

'I want to ask,' Pearl continued, 'if you will help us with the wall.'

'Of course,' I said. 'You won the debate.'

'I mean, on the planning side. You were the only one saying anything about the practicalities. What you said made me look again. I think five hundred yards is going to be too long.'

'I see.'

'We need something we can put up quickly and defend at all points. A longer wall means more potential areas of weakness. A shorter wall can be defended more easily. I'm thinking of reducing it. Three hundred yards. That would take us round the main buildings, though we'd have to give up the Lodge. We could keep the Lodge minimally stocked. I don't know, perhaps we could knock it down.'

So now Pearl was proposing to demolish parts of the school.

'I've also given some more thought to the height. Fourteen feet from ground level will be high enough, I think. Three feet in the ground. Seventeen feet altogether. If the inner walkway goes all the way round we'll still have a considerable height advantage.'

'What do you want me to do?'

'Well, first of all,' said Pearl, 'I want you to take a more detailed survey of the trees. I'd like you to look at heights and diameters and approximate weights and so on, given the new perimeter length and height. I can give you someone to help you. Titty, here.'

'Oh, no,' Titty said immediately.

'Don't you want to do it?' asked Pearl.

'I don't know anything about trees.'

'Stephen can teach you about trees,' said Tom, giggling.

'I'm sure he can,' said Titty with a hard stare. 'He can also teach you about trees.'

'Come on,' said Pearl reprovingly to Titty. 'This would be good for you.'

'What do you mean?' asked Titty.

'You know, in the elections. You could be a deputy.'

'I don't want to be a deputy.'

'All right, do it for me,' said Pearl.

'Why?'

'Because I think you owe me an apology.'

Titty furrowed her brows. 'What for?'

Pearl looked hard at her. 'For calling me a dwarf. Do you still think I'm a dwarf?'

Although certainly dwarfish, Pearl stood as though she were fourteen feet high, with three in the ground. Determination of an almost supernatural order blazed from her tiny eyes and grey cheeks.

Titty looked at her for a while, and then, reddening, cast her eyes down. 'All right,' she said. 'I'll help, if that's what you want.'

And so, one morning, Titty and I took a walk in the woods. I say we walked. Internally, I danced. I had never been alone with Titty before.

The weather was cool, with a low fog rolling in from the east. Titty was wearing her school skirt with a brown-and-yellow laterally-striped tank-top, from home. The tank-top fitted her very tightly. I kept a good two paces from her at all times.

The western half of the island, in which the school was situated, was relatively untreed, having just a few sparse pines dotted about. To reach the forest, one walked to the top of the low ridge that cut the island in half. Here, much of the tree-cover had been burnt, but the damage hadn't spread more than a dozen yards down the hill. Looking a quarter of a mile to the sea, one could see the plantation in all its glory. I'd always loved to linger at the ridge and look out towards Wideopen and Sonnet. Since the school's founding, many of the original trees had seeded new ones, expanding the plantation to cover the whole of the eastern portion of the island. In some places, groves of young trees crowded densely with only a couple of feet between them. Here there was still light beneath the feathery boughs. It was only in the older parts of the wood, to which we now descended, that gloom and silence truly reigned.

'I've lived here my whole life,' I said, gesturing around me. 'I know this place like the back of my hand.' I slapped a tree. 'Do you know that this tree is a hundred years old?'

'No, I don't,' said Titty dully.

'There are three conifers native to Britain,' I said. 'The Scots pine, the yew and the juniper. These are Scots pine.'

'Really.'

'Seabirds won't nest here, of course. But we get some other birds. Like jays. I can do their calls if you like. Do you want to hear a jay?'

'Not particularly.'

'It's really life-like.'

'If you insist.'

I gave my best jay impression. A jay makes a hoarse, guttural screech. I took care to face away from Titty. Jays produce a lot of saliva.

Titty's eyes became a little rounder. She gave me a half smile. It was the most amused expression I'd ever seen her make. Seeing it was like the first time I had tried a cigarette, when my head had filled with tingling clouds of unreason.

'It's better if I get up a tree and do it,' I said. 'Then you can't see me. You'd think it was the real thing.'

'I'm sure you're right,' she said.

'Male jays give their partner food as a courtship ritual.'

'Like what?'

'Chocolates,' I said.

'How can they give chocolates?'

'Plenty of people throw chocolates out at Christmas. The jays store them up and ration them out through the year.'

'That's very enterprising of them.'

'Titty. I want to tell you something.'

'What?'

'I know you don't want to be here.'

'So?'

'We don't need to go through all this measuring. There's something else we can do.'

'What?'

I gulped. 'Come with me to the mainland.'

Titty frowned.

'Come with me to the mainland,' I repeated. 'We can find out what happened. Pearl is crazy. We can't build this wall. If we don't leave, we'll die here. There's a big world out there. It can't all be obliterated. Do you want to die here?'

'What do you mean, come to the mainland? How?'

'By boat. The beast-man's boat. I'll row. I'm strong. I know the tides.'

'I thought you agreed to abide by the debate. That means building the wall.'

'No! I was lying. Why would I do that?'

Titty stood still and regarded me. It didn't seem to be a very positive regard, but at least it was a regard.

'Why are you asking me, in particular?' she said.

'You don't want to die here. When we get there, we'll travel. In secret, at night. We'll find out what happened to your family.'

'Other girls have families,' said Titty. 'Why don't you ask them? What about Laura? She and Pearl can't stick each other. If anyone would go, she would. She said it herself.'

'Laura can't stick me either.'

'Why not?'

'She's a snob. She's a rich girl. It's because my dad was Spanish. She's a racialist.'

Titty made a face. It seemed to express the feeling that although it was distasteful that Laura was a racialist, there was nothing anyone could really do about it.

'The thing is,' I said, 'my dad could be richer than her dad. Maybe he's from a really noble family or something. Maybe he's a Moorish king. Maybe he's still alive. I should be in Spain right now, with a harem.'

'What's a harem?'

'It's a collection of women.'

Titty made a noise. 'That's funny.'

'Why?'

'Because that's what you've got here.'

It was true. I had Mary-Dot, and Zillah, and Karen Dworkin, and Bettina Farque, and Bee, and Paula Ott, and Amber Wells, and Eufemia Paleocapa, and Barbara Pulmow, and Anne Heaviside, and forty-four other girls who were nothing like a harem and more like my sisters. Though I suppose any member of a harem might be someone's sister.

I could think of no very witty counter to Titty's insight. I suppose true wit consists of making clever connections. I didn't have any.

'A harem is for women you have sex with,' I said crudely. 'What else do you think they're for?'

'That's boring,' said Titty.

An ugly silence descended.

'All right,' I said. 'My father probably doesn't have a harem. If he has I wouldn't want to inherit it.'

The sea roared faintly. Our walk had slowed to a crawl. Titty padded cat-like on the brown needles.

'I don't know anything about my father, actually,' I continued. 'He was something to do with museums, but I don't know what. My mum never talked about him, and I didn't ask. I should have asked. It's just that I never did.'

I had chosen the worst possible girl in the school to fall in love with. Out of an entire harem I had fastened on the one guaranteed to make me unhappy.

'All right, said Titty. 'Let's get back to your problem. You want to get away and you need someone to go with you. That's right, is it?'

'Yes.'

'Okay. How about Beulah?'

'Too bossy.'

'Pamela?'

'Too weedy. I'd need someone to take turns rowing.'

'I thought you were going to do it.'

'I am. It's just that I'll need a break once in a while. But I'll do most of it. Ninety-five percent. Ninety-nine.'

Titty didn't seem anywhere near agreeing, but she hadn't said no yet. At this point I felt it advisable to play my trump card.

'It's a risk,' I said. 'We might drown. And maybe the mainland does have packs of hungry crazed murderers roaming everywhere. Murderesses too. I'm looking for someone who would take a risk. That's you. I don't offer you certainty. I offer you a hazardous journey, constant danger. Safe return doubtful. Honour and recognition in case of success.'

I doubted if she recognised the quote from Ernest Shackleton. Nevertheless, as I anticipated, she perked up.

'I appreciate the offer, Stephen,' she said. 'I do, honestly. But you don't need me. You can do it on your own. Give me one good reason why you need me to go with you.'

I licked my lips. 'Because you want to. Because you want to find out about your family. Think about it. Don't answer now.'

Of course I had no intention of rowing to the mainland. Getting as far as Wideopen had nearly led to four deaths. If I never stepped into a rowboat again it would be too soon. But since Titty was impractical, temperamental, humourless, vindictive, and mad, unable to see which side her bread was buttered on and with a tendency to cut off her nose to spite her face, it was advantageous to pretend that Pearl was a fool.

That afternoon I went to Pearl's office on the ground floor of the Lodge to deliver my report. Titty had declined to accompany me.

'I've put it in writing,' I said, handing Pearl a couple of sheets of paper.

'Summary, please,' said Pearl.

I withdrew my sheets. 'All right. Well, your estimate of ten thousand trees is about right. Half of these are young. Or at least adolescent. You could call them second-generation. They're tall, though – about thirty feet, on average.'

'Good. We'll strip off the tops and perhaps the base, depending on the width. We'll need to go for an average width of about six inches, to cut down on weight.'

'Okay.'

'Now. How many could we cut and trim a day, do you think?' Pearl asked.

'I don't know. It would depend how many girls were doing it, and for how long.'

'I'm thinking about ten staves a day. Does that seem about right to you?'

'Possibly.'

'You don't seem very certain.'

'No, I'm not. I don't know how hard it will be to cut down ten trees a day.'

'All right. We'll experiment. Now, if we cut ten staves a day, and put them up the same day, how long will it take to make a 300-yard wall?'

'Well, tens into...'

'It's a hundred and eighty days, Stephen.'

'Yes, something like that.'

'Exactly like that. Of course, we'll also have to dig trenches, build walkways and so on.' Pearl grinned. 'Would you like a cup of tea? I'm sure there's still some around somewhere. Milk powder, of course. We do have sugar if you want it.'

I was surprised. Elizabeth Pelham had told us that all the tea and sugar were gone.

'Yes, please,' I said.

'All right. Henry!'

Henry appeared via an interconnecting door.

'Stephen would like a cup of tea. One sugar.'

Henry nodded and left the room.

'Good. Well, that was very useful,' said Pearl. 'I hope Titty helped you.'

'Yes,' I said. 'She was very... helpful.'

'Good. She needs to take some responsibility. I want you to be happy, you know. You're a very important part of this school. In fact we really couldn't do without you.'

'Oh. Thank you.'

'So you're on our side, now? About the wall?'

'Yes. I agreed to abide by the result of the debate.'

Pearl nodded slowly.

'And I want you to know,' I went on, 'that actually… I do agree with you. We have to protect ourselves. Bows and arrows aren't enough.'

'No, they're not.'

Henry arrived with the tea. It was delicious. I was reminded of bedtimes before the war. As a child, I used to drink two cups of tea a night. One to drink quickly, and one to drink slowly, as I used to say to my mother.

'Well,' said Pearl. 'I'm drawing up a new timetable and I think we can start early next week. We'll need to make the most of the summer.'

I finished my tea. 'That was very nice,' I said.

'Don't tell the others we still have any left,' Pearl said, writing something.

Have you ever made a bow? As in bows and arrows? Of course you have. So many have, these days. We live in the age of Einstein.

Unfortunately, the only available wood on Near was, as discussed, pine. Though durable, light and easy to work, pine is not a very dense wood, and so not particularly suitable for bows. When made thin enough to bend, a pine bow will splinter.

Our bowmistress-in-chief was Fritzi Pietsch from Hamm (or Fritzi Hamm from Pietsch). I have mentioned Fritzi's role in harvesting the unsuitable tern population. Fritzi had a certain air of Teutonic practicality about her. One could imagine her in lederhosen in the Black Forest, making fire by rubbing sticks together. Fritzi was also beautiful, with golden hair and lips like cinema seats. Beauty is a strange thing. One can recognise it without being attracted by it.

In the basement were some flexible plastic tubes left over from an electrical refurbishment. Fritzi discovered that when a pine limb was stuffed into one of these tubes, the whole could be bent without the wood splintering. The resulting weapon was light, flexible and powerful. Arrows could be made from pine sticks with fire-hardened tips, fledged with tern feathers.

Archery supplied some of the spirit that up till then had been lacking among the girls. Competitions were organised. Targets, made out of cardboard boxes packed with old newspapers, were set up. Girls were given marks for accuracy and penetration. Fritzi organised the tournaments, with small prizes awarded to the most skilled.

We soon progressed to the shooting of live targets: seabirds and rabbits. Rabbits lived in large numbers on the island, but their burrows were deep, and they fled at the sight of a human. They could, however, be taken with bows. I tried my hand at rabbit-murder, but not with any relish. It was pitiful to see a rabbit attempting to run with an arrow poking out of it.

Girls would queue for bows and arrows in the morning, go hunting, and return the weapons, with any quarry, at lunchtime. Those who provided meat were awarded house points; and at the end of the month the winning house would be conferred certain privileges. As a result of Bee Wasket's bloodlust, Wideopen were allowed to wear rabbit-skin caps.

I have mentioned vegetables. Haven't I? Well, if I haven't, something must be said about them.

At first, nothing grew very well. The crops had survived the war, to be sure, but they were yellow of leaf and paltry of root.

A council meeting was held, consisting of the four captains plus their deputies. Char Parr and Bettina Farque were called in to testify as expert witnesses. I sat in as recorder.

Char Parr was of the opinion that the crops were doing poorly due to low temperatures. Bettina concurred. Paula Ott, as the deputy of Brownstone, suggested a greenhouse. Bettina pointed to the lack of spare glass. Mary-Dot Golding proposed the removal of all the sash windows from the upper floor of the Shute Building. A vote decided the matter. Thirty-four sash windows were to be removed. The unglazed gaps would then be either boarded over or supplied with shutters that could be latched in the evening or during rain.

This was where I lived, so I felt a little put out.

The greenhouse was constructed just outside the assembly hall, within the ambit proposed for the new 300-yard stockade. The greenhouse was about thirty feet long, triangular, with a central ridge-pole. The sash windows were set into a frame designed to retain them under their own weight, then tacked in place. There being no putty available, earth was mixed with fulmar-oil to produce a sticky substance that could be applied to any gaps.

Inside the greenhouse, five main crops were cultivated: potatoes, cabbage, carrots, rosehips and onions. The rosehips were to supply vitamin C, and were added whole to stews.

Given a few extra degrees of warmth, and fed with Murray Mint's manure, the crops prospered. And they were certified free from radioactivity, since they were supplied with pure Near water from Pearl's well.

Thus, our island-originating foodstuffs were a mixture of root crops, leafy crops, hips, rabbit, fulmar and puffin. No seal had yet died for the colony, though one probably still had a headache. Sealskin would be useful at some point for hats, boots, clothes and tents. Seal meat would be good to eat. And the fat could be rendered into oil for lamps – if we ever ran out of fulmar – or cooking.

The beast-man had become somewhat unkempt in the three months he'd been in his cage. He was very hairy, his clothes were filthy with mud, and his cage was spotted all over with guano. He still nursed a wound to his manhood, the exact parameters of which were unknown, except to him.

No one had spoken to him in all that time. His life in our post-war settlement consisted of sitting wrapped in a blanket, unspeaking, unspoken-to and unspeakable.

Girls on watch had begun to observe him doing something strange. At odd moments, he would grip the end-bars of his cage and lean on them, making the cage creak a little to one side. Then he would desist, as if it were merely an accident. But then, on another watch, another girl would see him do the same, only in the opposite direction. It was clear that, unable to undo the bolts sunk by Bettina Farque, he was trying to loosen the joints. The news was related to Pearl.

I was there to see what happened next. It was a Thursday morning, before school, and the beast-man was sitting, as usual, on the bare earth, his back to the main pillar of the cage. As before, Pearl sat at a table positioned outside the ten-foot circle. This time she was alone at her table. The girls stood around to listen.

'Please answer me when I speak,' began Pearl, 'to show me that you understand. If you don't, you will be punished. Do you understand?'

The beast-man said nothing. He shifted a little in his filthy blanket.

'Do you understand what I'm saying to you?' asked Pearl again.

'Yes,' said the beast-man.

'Good. Firstly, is there anything you wish to tell us?' asked Pearl.

A Pearlish question.

'Yes,' the beast-man said. He cleared his throat. 'I'm sorry for what I did.'

Pearl nodded a little.

'I want to make you an offer,' he went on. 'You want to put up a wall. I've heard you talking. That was my idea, you remember. I can help you. I can do three times as much work as you. Four times. I can move logs. I can dig trenches.'

It was, I suppose, the most he'd said to anyone for months. Pearl said nothing.

'I've thought about it,' he continued. 'You can put me in chains or tie me to a tree. I can still work. You don't need to come anywhere near me. What I did was stupid. I've paid for that. I've paid!'

I felt that he had paid. Many of the girls must have felt the same. They were still soft-hearted girls, in spite of everything. In my experience girls of that age like fluffy things, like lambs and socialism. It was hard to watch a fellow human being suffer so greatly, and in plain sight. It was surely a form of torture. As Kat Egg would doubtless have said, had she been asked, torture was outlawed under the Geneva Convention.

'Have you finished?' Pearl said.

'Yes,' said the beast-man. 'Except to say I've learned my lesson. If you don't want me to work for you, then just put me back in my boat and I'll go. If you keep me here you've got to feed me and look after me. It'd be easier for you if I was just gone. I won't bother you again. And I won't tell anyone I was here.'

'I see,' said Pearl. 'That it?'

'Yes.'

'Very well,' Pearl said. 'Let me tell you, then, that we will *not* be doing any of the things you have just said.'

She paused as if to give him the chance to respond. But the beast-man just let his mouth hang open idiotically.

'You will *not* be released,' Pearl went on. 'We do not trust you. Neither do we need your help. You are a rapist and a liar. You will stay in that cage for as long as we think fit. By the time you get out we will be old women. And for as long as you are in that cage, no one will speak to you, because you do not deserve to be spoken to.'

The beast-man gave her a look of pure hate.

'Do you understand what I'm saying?' Pearl said.

The beast-man then said some words that must be redacted from the present narrative. This is, after all, an adventure story set on a desert island, not a pornographic tract.

'It has come to our attention,' said Pearl, ignoring him, 'that you have been trying to damage your cage. You are not permitted to do this. In fact, from now on, you are not permitted to touch the bars of your cage at any time. You may not sit with your back on the pillar as you are doing at the moment. If you wish to sit or lie down, you will do so on your bed. Any attempt to touch any of the other wooden members of the cage will be met with swift punishment. Do you understand?'

'You're a little whore.'

Pearl got up from her chair. 'Good. I'm glad we understand one another.'

But the beast-man had bounded to his feet, thrown off his blanket and rushed to the bars, gripping them tightly with both hands.

'I'll get out of here,' he slavered, eyes wide. 'Someone will find me. They'll come for me. I'll tell them what you did. Then I'll kill you myself.'

And there followed a string of obscenities not notable for their originality, but unmatched for desperate vehemence, issuing from the soul of a Benn Gunn whose idée fixe was rape instead of toasted cheese.

Pearl stood and listened. 'That is the last time you touch those bars. Whenever anyone on watch sees you do it again, you will be punished. Fisher,' she added.

The beast-man slid down the bars and gave a terrible howl of rage, of pain and despair. I recalled what Alexandra Featherstonehaugh had said during the debate on his execution: 'But if we start with murder we'll be starting with something evil.'

This imprisonment seemed almost as evil as murder.

As Pearl had promised, the new timetable was inaugurated soon after our meeting in the Lodge. I don't remember any debate being held.

Whereas the pre-war timetable had included subjects such as German, Geography, English, Maths and Biology, the new timetable dispensed with languages (as unlikely to be of much use in our altered circumstances), humanities (as unlikely to be of much use in our altered circumstances) and sciences (as unlikely to be of much use in our altered circumstances). Instead it comprised the following seven subjects: Repairs, Horticulture, Hunting, Fortifications 1, Fortifications 2, Fortifications 3, and Catering. It was organised in quadruple periods, with whole mornings or afternoons given over to a particular subject. Thus, those who had been studying Catering in the morning were able to feed the Hunters at lunch; and those who had worked hard on Forti in the morning were given a break with Horti in the afternoon.

The classes were organised by house, as in pre-war days. Teachers, it soon became evident, were unnecessary. The captains of house (Pearl, Robyn, Mary-Dot and Amber), aided by their deputies (Tom Keck, Paula Ott, Francesca Mond and Polly Findhorn) were each able to take six or seven girls and allot tasks. A planning meeting was held on Saturday evenings after class, and special dinners, as I have mentioned, were held thrice a week in the Lodge. Sundays were off. Except prayers.

Forti 1, 2 and 3 were the core of the curriculum. Every weekday morning, a single house – let us say Mancoe, for purposes of illustration – would study Forti 1. This was a practical subject. It involved digging a trench four and a half feet long, two feet wide and three feet deep, with a special cross-section like a 'U' with a crooked side. The lower, six-inch-wide part of the bottom of the trench was designed to receive the stave. At any one time three girls would dig, three bucket away spoil, and the rest wait their turn to do either. Ten minutes was generally enough for each turnaround, making progress rapid, as each girl was fresh to the task. Nevertheless a trench of the specified dimensions would generally take about three hours, which would bring the girls up to lunch.

Meanwhile, on that same weekday morning, another house, let us say Wideopen, would be studying Forti 2. This was also a practical subject. It involved cutting, trimming and delivering (with the aid of the equine) nine staves (one less than Pearl's ten), each seventeen feet long and six inches in diameter. These dimensions had to be exact, particularly the diameter, since these nine staves had to fit snugly into the four-and-a-half-foot trench the team had dug that morning. Nine times six inches is four and a half feet. A truth as old as Osiris.

In the afternoon these two teams would occupy themselves with Repairs and Horti, occupations involving painting, screwing, nailing, sawing, laddering, cleaning, bucketing, digging, wheelbarrowing, pruning, harvesting, watering, planting, weeding and potting. But the real brute labour would now be undertaken by those studying Forti 3.

Forti 3, on any given afternoon, would be studied simultaneously by two houses – say Darling and Brownstone – comprising in total twenty-eight girls. This was also a practical subject. It involved placing the seventeen-foot staves into the four-and-a-half-foot trench, then back-filling it with stones and earth, making sure the fence was true to the vertical. This was done with ropes, Murray Mint, and a backstop frame constructed by Bettina Farque.

Each stave would begin its ordeal laid on the ground, its base in the trench and its tip raised onto a three-foot trestle at the halfway point. A hole would be drilled in the stake about two feet from the tip. A rope, passing through this hole and secured at the back, would run up to the backstop placed at the far edge of the trench. This rope would then be attached to Murray Mint, who, at the word of command from his handler (MM was a very intellectual animal), would raise each stave into position. Guy-ropes from left to right would be held by four girls apiece to ensure that the stave did not swing to either side as it was being pulled upright.

After the first stave had been placed and secured, the main rope, still through the eye of the first stave, would be pulled back and attached to the second stave, in the familiar supine position. The second stave would then be pulled up to join the first. When all nine staves had been placed and backfilled, the day's work was done.

The process would repeated the following day. *Videlicet*: a ditch would be dug in the morning by one house, staves selected and prepared by another, and the staves placed in the afternoon by the remaining two. At the end of two days' work a nine-foot panel was accordingly completed, comprising eighteen staves. This panel was then tied through the holes with an inch-thick dowel. Reinforcing beams were placed horizontally at the back, on one of which rested (later) a walkway.

Subsequent nine-foot panels were constructed in much the same way, except that it was now possible to dispense with the backstop. Instead, a six-inch buffer was mounted on the near edge of the nine-foot panel, enabling Murray Mint to pull the staves up through their respective eyes without binding on the first panel. This six-inch gap would then be infilled with a final stave at the end of two days.

I hope this is helpful to you in the construction of your own fortifications.

Some of the smaller girls were under four feet tall and as wiry as carpet fluff. The average height was perhaps five feet. Many of the girls tended to cut, bruise, sprain or graze themselves or others. Some seemed to take too literally the adage 'Always cut towards your friend'.

At first, then, progress was not as rapid as the ideal scenario I have outlined above.

The most hazardous moment during Forti 3 was probably the erection of the final stave between each panel, since it had to be accomplished laterally. Here the buffers were removed and the backstop frame would be brought into service again, this time at a ninety-degree angle to the trench. The stave, having no trench walls to restrain its motion from side to side, had to be securely held left and right before slotting it into position.

The following incident happened, I suppose, at some point in September, a month after the wall was begun.

It was late in the afternoon and getting dark. Eleven tired girls (and your narrator) were on rope-duty, holding the stave in position as Murray Mint pulled it from the trestle to the upright, led by Lisa Plast. Robyn Loss-Stevenson supervised with clip-board and pen.

At first, the stave seemed to be sliding into place as planned. But at about forty-five degrees of elevation the base of the stave slipped sideways and out of the hole, riding forward and out of control. The sudden loss of tension on the ropes caused the stave to skew sideways in the gap. The girls scrambled to escape the falling stave, but one girl was not quick enough. The stave caught her a smart blow to the head. That girl was Minna Bye.

Robyn ran over to her, gripping her clipboard close to her chest. Minna was stretched out on the ground like a shoe-flattened spider. There was no mark on her. She looked like she would never move again.

'Is she breathing?' asked Mickey Kodiak.

Hillary Kaplan put her hand in front of Minna's mouth. 'I think so,' she said. 'It's warm.'

'Someone get Pearl,' said Joy Sadd.

'I'll go,' I said.

I ran the short distance to the Lodge. Darling were on Hunting that afternoon but I had seen them come back. Pearl would be busy with something.

I burst into her office. 'It's Minna,' I shouted.

Pearl was at her desk listening to a record-player. She frowned. 'What?'

'She's been knocked unconscious.'

Pearl got to her feet. She still seemed to be attending to the music. 'Were you using the backstop?' she asked.

'Yes,' I said.

'Put her on a plank and stretcher her here. We'll make up one of the teachers' rooms. Is she breathing?'

'Yes.'

'Okay, let's go. You run first and I'll join you.'

I ran from the room. But as I got to the doorway, I paused and looked over my shoulder. Pearl was unhurriedly putting on her coat. She still hadn't turned off the record player, which was playing something classical, though I couldn't identify it. It might have been Bruckner.

I then heard what Pearl said under her breath.

'Thank God it was Minna.'

Pearl's remark about Minna was shocking, but, the more I thought about it, the more I understood it. From a practical perspective.

Minna wasn't a rich girl like Laura Huxley. She wasn't a scholar like Robyn Loss-Stevenson. Nor was she sporty like Karen Dworkin, strong like Zillah Smith, religious like Char Parr, eccentric like Jules Cashford, or good-looking like Fritzi Pietsch from Hamm (or Fritzi Hamm from Pietsch). Nor was she a person with any sincere interest in anything aside from the occasional frivolous scheme that everyone (including her) knew would come to nothing.

A few girls, frightened by Minna's injury, would inevitably question the necessity of the wall, but they could easily be brought back into the fold. If Pamela Gowler or Deedee Foe or someone popular had been injured, it would have been a disaster. As it was, it was just Minna. Minna was just Titty's

121

friend. Why Titty bothered with her no one could say. She was an index of Titty's perversity.

Minna did not die on that first day. Her head ballooned and she did not regain consciousness. Kat Egg, who wanted to be a doctor, advised alternating cold and hot compresses, which had the virtue of possibly being right fifty percent of the time.

Neither did Minna die on the second day. The teacher's room at the Lodge – formerly Miss Steel's, of Chemistry and Sports fame – was ideal, being hushed, supplied with posters of drowned women, and remote from the girls' dormitories.

On the third day Minna recovered consciousness, rolled her eyes at the ceiling, then sank back into her coma.

On the fourth day Minna woke fully and looked round her. On the fifth, she was sufficiently recovered to drink some soup, but refused to talk. And during the next days and weeks, when addressed, she seemed not to hear. If I hadn't known about her injury I would have said she was merely depressed.

Here I should explain one particular circumstance of her accident. The toppling of the stave, and its disastrous concomitant, had been witnessed not only by the girls of Brownstone (and myself) but by one other person. A male person. The beast-man's cage was quite near the section of wall being erected on that dim afternoon. When I ran to the Lodge I passed within ten feet of him. I saw his head turn a little as I ran. I was aware of his gaze, though I did not meet it. Nor, of course, did I address him.

I felt him thinking. 'Well, sonny-boy, is this how you handle an island-full of girls? What kind of a boy are you?'

And here the sequel to the meeting between Pearl and the beast-man must be related.

The beast-man, for about a week, did all that Pearl had asked of him. He did not touch the bars. He remained on his bed, sleeping his life away. But after a week, it was reported – by Maud Colby, on watch in the small hours – that he had begun to lean, as before, on the supporting members of his cage.

Pearl was apprised of the situation, and called a council meeting. I did not attend it. I had been on Forti 2 in the afternoon and I wanted to lie on my bed with a book. Our library was well stocked with post-apocalyptic literature. In fact, all of it was post-apocalyptic literature. It was Robyn who informed me that the punishment of the beast-man would take place the following morning. The whole school would be expected to attend, at ten o'clock by the front of the Shute Building.

I spent an uneasy night. I did not like the idea of punishing the beast-man. I felt, somehow, he was being punished as much for being a man as for being a beast.

In the morning I joined the throng of expectant girls near the beast-man's cage. Pearl and the three captains had already taken up their places. Just next to them stood Fritzi.

Fritzi wore what must have been a former teacher's garment, a white silk blouse with a red sash. The blouse was cut low and her breasts stood out. Her hair, golden and loose, sported small roses, and perched on her head was a rabbit-skin cap. Her eyes and lips had been made up with cosmetics. In one hand she carried a bow, and on her back she wore a quiver of arrows. On her left arm she wore a suede-leather arm-guard. She stood there stringing and testing her bow.

Pearl stood up from her place near the ten-foot circle. She addressed the beast-man in his malodorous prison.

'It has come to our attention that you disregarded the instructions given to you last week. The council has decided on your punishment.'

Everyone suddenly realised what Fritzi was doing there. There were purrs of excitement.

'You will be dealt a punitive wound,' Pearl said curtly. She sat down.

The beast-man snarled something. Then he got to his feet. With an effort, he picked up his bed, turning it so it stood on its foot. He placed it between himself and Fritzi.

Pearl nodded to Fritzi. Fritzi advanced in a stately walk towards the cage. She stopped about two yards from the bars, and began to walk around it. The beast-man hastily repositioned his bed. But it was heavy, and it cost him some effort. Fritzi continued to circle. He ducked behind the bed, trying to evade her. Fritzi unhurriedly walked the full circle back to the place where she had started. Laughter began. Fritzi smirked and held her bow up over her head. The laughter and cheers rose. She began her walk again, slow and deliberate. The beast-man scrabbled. Then Fritzi, feinting suddenly to one side, drew her bow and loosed an arrow through the bars. It struck the beast-man's right thigh. The arrow seemed to penetrate a good couple of inches, and stuck and trembled there. The beast-man gave an agonised cry and fell to the ground.

The girls screamed.

Pearl and the captains of house stood up. The beast-man, sprawling in the dirt, his face contorted, gripped the arrow and pulled it from his leg. A little plume of blood spurted out. He moved his lips to say something, but whatever he said was drowned in screams.

Pearl clapped her hands, and the crowd quieted. 'Antibiotics will be put in your food,' she announced.

My last memory of the incident is a crowd of admiring girls around Fritzi. They were very curious about her clothes.

THREE

How is radiation sickness where you are? Is your hair falling out? Are your gums bleeding? How are you doing in your life generally?

How are the seabirds where you are? Tasty? And how are the seals? Compliant? How is your water, and your rain? How are your family, your loved ones? Your walls and ditches? Your stores and hidden places? How are your nests and burrows, your Robinsonian retreats? Life is a cavalcade, or a Robinsonade.

When I saw the girls – my fellow students – laughing and screaming as a human being was being tortured, I did begin to wonder whether our little project was in good health. We had lost the Anglican Church, Boots the Chemist, the Fire Brigade, the Independent Nuclear Deterrent, Radio 4, BBC1 and BBC2. And ITV. We had, in psychoanalytic terms, lost the restraining power of the superego. Had we, as a result, fallen victim to the promptings of the Id?

How are your graves?

August turned to September, which turned to October. By the end of October, the wall was about two-fifths completed. That is, we'd put up a hundred and thirty-five yards of it. It began opposite the sports block, went down to the Lodge, made a ninety-degree right-hand turn, went past the beast-man's cage and across the front of the Shute Building, and then halted just before the second corner.

In October Pearl began marking out the ground for a ditch outside the wall. This measure would keep any berserking rapists a further twelve feet away. If they approached any nearer, they could be shot by girls up on the walkway. The walkway also afforded excellent views of said rapists before they were able to present a danger, and excellent views withal of the coast, where rapist-rowboats might be seen arriving.

The girls were now very proficient at hunting. All the seabirds had been tested, and many had been adjudged fit for the table. Near, as I have pointed out, was a bird sanctuary of national, if not international, importance. Or rather, it *had* been a sanctuary. Now it was a larder.

We still had multitudes of rabbits and a reasonable supply of vegetables. The freezers had been emptied, but about a quarter of the pre-war non-perishable stores remained: seemingly endless supplies of Biba Baked Beans and Bird's Raspberry Instant Whip. However, we had still not bagged a seal. Seals are full of vitamins. Accordingly, in late October, during a clement spell, a hunting party was once again assembled. Once again, I was chosen to take part.

I have previously said that nothing could have persuaded me to get into a row-boat again. Perhaps I should have added 'except Pearl'.

Pearl called Robyn and myself to the Lodge for a special lunch on the 25th October. She congratulated us on Brownstone's work that month, particularly given that we were a girl down (with the loss of Minna, who had still not recovered sufficiently to participate). She told us that the opening of a seal fishery was of paramount importance for the survival of the school. She said that only I had the experience and knowledge to navigate the treacherous waters around

Wideopen. She said that she would regard it as a great personal favour if I would consent. She asked Robyn if she could spare me. Robyn replied that she could.

Pearl did *not* say that she would, in return for this favour, cease to make reference in public utterances to the male half of humanity being diseased and unregenerable.

My team-mates were, as before, chosen for their strength. Bee Wasket was once again selected. Bee had a quite masculine appetite for death.

Karen Dworkin and Zillah Smith were replaced by Kay Hawkins and Char Parr.

Kay Hawkins I had always regarded as disturbed. Her hair was cut high over a towering forehead and she was a fanatical pencil-chewer, often stripping the wood down to the lead. The apocalypse had entirely cured her of this habit, since she now never went near a pencil.

Char Parr was a religious girl with an unnaturally fleshy nose, unnaturally fleshy lips, and unnaturally fleshy eyes. She was the school's head gardener, and thus one of the girls more conducive to our survival. This was the party line, anyhow. But who really misses a gardener?

As I looked at my companions in the hunt, I could not help but think that if we all drowned the school would go on much the same. No one would miss me, certainly. Titty was as aloof as ever.

This time we pushed off at six in the morning. We aimed to be back the same day. I insisted on this, not wishing to share a tent with Bee, Char and Kay.

Instead of making directly for Wideopen, we set off from the north-east shore of Near, then rowed hard in an easterly direction, seeking to get a good way out before crossing the current and being pulled back to Wideopen. The strategy worked well. We rowed hard for about two hours, met the stream flowing between the two islands, and within another hour, at about nine o'clock, were beaching up on Wideopen's northern shore.

As we walked to the seal-grounds, I began to feel anxious. Why had we failed the last time? Were seals, in fact, killable? Were they somehow too padded to be bludgeoned?

I eyed Bee, striding along in front of us, occasionally taking practice shots on boulders. Did she have the strength of arm actually to do the deed? And if not, would I be required to do it?

We rounded the headland. The seals lay before us in their blubbery congregations. Bee walked up to the nearest one, hammer in hand. It was a middling-looking seal, whitish with ashy flecks. Bee took a stance over it and gazed full into its mild eyes. She raised the hammer and brought it down hard on the seal's head. The seal hit the ground like a dropped water-balloon.

Bee squatted over the prone seal and inspected it. Taking it gently under its jaw, she lifted its head and let it drop. She did this again. She seemed to consider for a while. Then she raised her hammer once more. Still squatting, and with a hard-breathing, systematic violence, she began bludgeoning the seal's skull. Thunk, thunk. On the third or fourth blow, blood began to spray from the seal's nose and mouth. Bee continued hammering. Blood spattered over her shoes and socks. Then her hands and face.

Bee stood up. I hesitate to describe the state of that seal. It was, shall we say, tenderised.

Bee looked back at us with an unfocussed stare that seemed to say: 'You want to eat seal-meat? Well, this is how it is done.'

We then took the seal by its tail and dragged it to the boat, leaving a crimson track.

I hoped it wasn't the same one she'd picked on last time. That would have been deeply unfair.

The voyage back went as planned. On landing, we put the seal in a wheelbarrow and rolled it back to the school via the forest track.

The seal was gutted and flayed, and its skin scraped clean of blubber. The skin itself was as thick as shoe leather: it was stretched on a wooden frame by Bettina Farque. Then the meat, blubber, guts and bone were separated and examined. The bones were boiled clean and the water drunk as soup. Half the meat was casseroled, and the rest packed in salt.

Seal-meat is extremely tasty. As for flavour, seal might be termed the venison of the sea. This would argue that the deer is the seal of the land. The meat is very dark and rich, and the fat pervades all parts of the meat, making it tender.

The guts, although probably edible, were given to the birds. Teenage girls are strange about guts.

October turned to November. On November 21st, the first snows fell. Up above, on the ridge, the burnt-out skeletons of the pines were dusted white. The sun, visible as a vague aureole behind the clouds, hung low on the horizon, winking out at four o'clock.

Two sides of the beast-man's cage had been boxed over to give him respite from the wind. A one-man tent and sleeping bag had been added to his possessions, by decree of the council. Most of the time, therefore, he was invisible inside it, beneath a mound of blankets.

Forti was halted, to resume in the spring. A hundred and fifty yards of wall had been completed, exactly half the required length.

Food for the winter had been laid up in readiness. Attention now shifted to heating. In pre-war days the dormitories had been warmed by electric radiators. Now this was impossible.

Under the supervision of Pearl, we brought the dormitory beds together and crowded into smaller spaces. It's surprising how much heat a girl gives off. We ate a lot and stayed in our beds. We put blankets on the floor and over the windows and doors. We held blankets on the ceiling with bamboo poles, our own Sino-Bedouin tents. We hunted and abolished draughts. We drank hot water with rosehip.

We also gave thought to winter clothing. At the time of the war, two-thirds of the school had been absent, and they had left behind their spare uniforms plus their coats, jackets, jumpers, leggings, tights, cardigans, underwear and socks, as well as their home-wear. This included skirts, blouses, jeans, T-shirts, tank-tops, satchels, shoes and boots. The teachers too had left behind substantial wardrobes, including more exotic items: trench coats, fur coats, pants suits, suede skirts, high-heeled shoes, knee-length boots, canvas sneakers, pumps, sandals, jewellery, leather jackets, handbags, and even, in one case, a saree.

Pearl's highly popular decision was to turn all this clothing over to the captains. The girls had seen Fritzi's outfit – Artemis to the beast-man's ragged Actaeon – and everyone wanted the same opportunities to dress up.

School uniform was, accordingly, abolished. I would guess that this did more to cement Pearl's sovereignty than any other decision.

It was at first difficult to know how to apportion the clothing. After discussion in council, it was decided that clothing should be doled out by colour. Mancoe would be blue/green; Wideopen red/pink/purple; Brownstone brown/orange/yellow; and Darling black/white.

I say 'we' brought the dormitory beds together and 'we' apportioned the clothing. Actually I shivered in the Shute Building and took no part in pillaging the wardrobes. I had my school uniform, and plenty of coats. I moved my rooms down to the second floor, which still had some glazing, and there I stayed, emerging from bed for the occasional lavatory visit or blubber-snack.

On Sunday mornings, prayers were held in the assembly hall. This consisted first of a gospel reading, then an address by Pearl, and finally announcements by the captains or their deputies. Then a hymn.

At fifteen and a half years old, Pearl was not an awful lot bigger than she had been at fourteen. In fact she was meagre, shapeless and translucent, like a small boiled dumpling.

'Why are we putting up the wall?' she began, one Sunday before Christmas. She spoke, as usual, without notes. 'Well, you know the answer. For the same reason that the sun never shines. Men.'

True enough. Though I did not feel personally responsible.

'Unless we remember this, we won't survive here. Our survival depends on this truth. Men did this to us. And they will again.'

This was no news to her audience.

'War is biology,' Pearl continued. 'The gun and the atomic bomb are just extensions of men's flesh and men's minds.'

Pause. Serious face. Long nose, burning eyes. Gazing out into the beyond-Pearl.

'We're the lucky ones. We're protected from the worst they can do. By God's grace. In Matthew there's a verse: "For when you see the abomination of desolation standing where it ought not to be, then let those who are in Judea flee to the mountains." These islands are our mountains. Men are the abomination of desolation.'

Indeed.

'Men love weapons, you see. Men love swords, and guns, and tanks, and ships, and planes, and cannons, and bombs. Weapons are imagined by men, then made by men, then loved by men, then used by men. A man thinks of himself as a warrior with a sword. But the warrior with the sword is not the true face of war. The true face of war is a child by the body of her dead mother. And all because men love guns, and tanks, and bombs. And so, my dear friends, the only response to the death-drive of the male and the weapon-love of the male is to exclude him, to shun him, to shut him out, he whose nature brings these death-machines into the world.'

Pearl wound toward her peroration. She perorated. She sat down to the accompaniment of dutiful applause. A few girls rapped on the floor with their bow-stocks.

A hymn was sung: 'He who would valiant be'.

In a sense, I could see the necessity of it. If the girls hadn't been convinced of their imminent ravishment, would they have built the wall? And if they hadn't built the wall, what, actually, would they have done for the past year? Lain on their beds snivelling?

Outside, I bumped into Titty. She hadn't been present at prayers. Instead she was clearing snow from the front of the Shute Building.

'You managed to get out of that,' I said.

'I suppose,' said Titty. She looked spectacularly beautiful. Her cheeks were a fiery red and her hair was tied up at the back. Several strands had come loose and were fluttering in the wind.

'You didn't miss much,' I went on.

Titty stopped and rested both wrists on her broom. 'Why do you put up with it?' she asked.

'What?'

'Don't play the idiot.'

'It's Pearl's way of geeing us up,' I said.

'But it's not true, is it?'

From where we were standing we could see the beast-man in his cage. Most of the time he slept in his tent, but now he was up, draped in blankets, walking around. We could hear his low mumble on the morning air.

'Not in my case,' I said.

Titty returned to her sweeping. 'There was a time,' she said, 'when I thought there was more to you. I thought you wanted to get out of here. But actually you're Pearl's right-hand man, aren't you?'

I didn't say anything.

'You do whatever she wants. You help her with her wall. If she says "Get me a seal", you go and do it. Whenever she goes on about men, you get that look on your face. A little smile, like it's all true what's she's saying and please don't blame me for it, I'm a nice boy.'

'Well, what do you want me to do?' I asked.

She stopped again and pierced me with a look. 'I don't want you to do anything, Stephen. I don't care what you do.

But stop pretending that you're secretly planning something. You never wanted to go. Did you? That was just a lie.'

I felt like I had swallowed a fragment of seal-skull. 'I did…' I began.

'No, you didn't,' said Titty. Her glasses were at a crazy angle. 'You're lying now. Why do you always lie?'

'I…'

'I don't have any respect for liars,' she said, resuming her task.

The blood beat in my face. 'All right,' I blurted. 'I lied. All right? I said that because I wanted to impress you. I thought maybe you would come with me. And if you'd said yes, then maybe I *would* have gone to the mainland. I'd do anything for you. Don't you know that?'

I felt sick. I was Alison. I was Alison Barclay-Coutts. I had flayed every morsel of blubber from my soul.

Titty stood contemplating me. 'You just want to have sex with me,' she said finally. 'Then I'd have to have an abortion. There's no chance I'm risking that.'

'That's not true,' I said, not knowing if it were true or not.

'I don't care, Stephen,' Titty enunciated slowly, a terrifying gleam in her eye. 'Haven't I told you already? I'm not interested. I don't want anything to do with you! Do you understand what I'm saying?'

It was the question Pearl had asked the beast-man.

And so the truth, huge and useless, now lay between us, like a sofa left out in the rain.

Have you ever felt powerless? Of course you have.

But are you perhaps thinking: this boy has a school-full of girls at his disposal. He is in the right place at the right time, so to speak. Is it possible that, in such a fortunate situation, he will fixate on only one of them, to the exclusion of all the others... and not just fixate on one, but on the one who is the most inimical to him?

Is he really *that* perverse?

If such are your thoughts, how little you know of the human heart.

Winter passed slowly. Three things happened. The first concerned Barbara Pulmow. Barbara hadn't been able to participate in the construction of the wall, due to her asthma. After her medication ran out in September, she was confined to her room with her head over a bowl of steaming water.

Barbara was a thin girl with dark pouches under her eyes. Her disdain for the male sex – inculcated entirely by Pearl – was matched only by her love of *The Great Grape Ape Show*, a television cartoon featuring a twenty-foot-high purple gorilla that spends its time terrorising the general public.

Of course, now she couldn't watch the cartoon, but she had the comics.

We tried several remedies for Barbara's asthma, including one found in an ancient volume called *Dr Foote's Plain Medical Talk*. This called for onions. In the kitchen, we found a single wizened representative of this vegetable, covered in a greenish bloom. We scrubbed the bloom off. Then, as recommended in *Dr Foote's Plain Medical Talk*, we attached a string to it and suspended it from the ceiling. Barbara lay on her back on a table, and we set the onion rotating in small circles over her face.

As so often, the plain talk turned out to be barefaced lies.

After considerable wrestling with my own self-respect, I asked Barbara if she would like me to row her to the mainland to see if the requisite medications could be obtained. Of course, the likelihood of her being offered a pack of untampered salbutamol for anything less than her own body and soul was about as great as finding a fully-functioning chemist's shop complete with free vouchers and a courteous staff, but I thought it best to ask.

Looking me over sadly, she told me such a thing was unnecessary. My physique obviously did not match that of her hero, the Grape Ape: I had neither the strength of arm nor the hue of skin for the job. I am sure she knew I had only offered for form's sake. That pained me.

Barbara died in front of the entire school.

She had gone out to the refectory for lunch, which involved crossing from the dorms through the loggia to the main building. As she did so, clasping a soft toy of the Grape Ape, a bevy of hunters came shrieking and barrelling past her, chasing a rabbit that had emerged from a burrow outside the classrooms.

Some of the girls had not seen Barbara for weeks and may not have remembered what her particular malady entailed. 'Out of the way!' they screamed. Barbara, seeing their bows drawn, panicked and ran. After a few yards she collapsed on the grass, her chest heaving.

Girls crowded round her, offering advice. But Barbara, clutching at her Ape, eyes staring, suffocated.

Barbara's was the third death of the year, after my mother's and Yolanda Vane-Hovell-Vane's. She was interred next to them by the elm, not too far from where she had fallen.

The second development of the winter was that May Sussums, who had been ill, recovered and joined her peers. And Patsy Hugenoth, whose hair had fallen out, miraculously began growing it back again as thickly as before. No one knew why. Perhaps the damage being done by radioactive fallout from air or sea, or from eating irradiated birds, was being countered by the girls' natural healing mechanisms. Or perhaps the wind had just been blowing in the right direction.

You might also recall that in the previous year we only had a dozen bars of soap. They lasted about a month. A strange discovery was then made: everyone smells different. Some smell good, like fresh bread or rainy earth; and some smell bad, like stale oil or befouled shoes. A good person may smell bad, and a bad person may smell good. If a good person smells good, that is a confluence which, though accidental, will guarantee popularity; if a bad person smells bad, that is a confluence which, though equally accidental, will lead to her virtual excommunication.

Titty, though bad, smelled heavenly, like flowers.

Oneself, of course, has no smell whatever.

The third development concerned the forty-acre patch of land between the coast and the school. It was chiefly covered in heather and bracken – providing nesting sites for the visiting terns – but there were also several small stands of Scots pine, comprising altogether about two hundred trees. Pearl ordered these to be cut down so as not to give succour to the enemy. It was hard to imagine what succour the enemy could take from them.

In pre-war days it had been discovered – I remember the excitement it had caused at the time – that these stands of trees, and the tiny tarns beneath them, harboured a unique species of amphibian found only in the Near Islands. This creature was dubbed the Near Salamander. As already mentioned, a representation of the Near Salamander had made its way onto the school coat of arms, which featured dexter, a Near Salamander, and sinister, a puffin.

When the girls went out with axes and saws on fine January days to eliminate the offending trees, it was notable that no one mentioned the Near Salamander.

FOUR

Spring.

Anne Heaviside, high up on the unfinished wall, saw him first. A sailboat, making a zigzag course for Near. Breasting the waves, yoking the winds. A man, doing what men can do. She clomped off for Pearl, madly shouting.

When the sailboat put in, we were ready for it at the jetty. Twenty bows drawn; twenty quivers quivering. One wrong move and he would have looked like an orange on the cheese table at a buffet.

He was an older man, perhaps fifty. Tall and bald, flesh hanging in a way that suggested he'd once been stout. He wore a yellow oilskin with a dirty white scarf, and bell-bottomed jeans that obviously did not belong to him. He was shod in scuffed blue plastic sandals.

He tied his boat up quietly and stepped onto the jetty.

'Please put those bows down,' he said, raising his chin imperiously. 'You're liable to do someone an injury.'

Eyes flickered.

'I am Edward Vane-Hovell-Vane,' he said. 'Some of you may know me.'

It was Yolanda's father. The first father to arrive at the school, and it had to be Yolanda's. But I suppose it made sense. Yolanda had been Head Girl, after all. You would expect the father of a Head Girl to make more effort.

Pearl stepped forward. 'Please forgive the precautions,' she said. 'I'm afraid we had a bad experience with someone from the mainland.'

'I see,' said Mr Vane-Hovell-Vane.

'I'll order most of the bows to stand down,' Pearl said. She turned to the girls. 'Bows of Wideopen only.'

Fifteen girls lowered their bows. But the matter of bows and arrows, and of the unfortunate experience this little girl was referring to, or indeed any other issue, were subordinate to the one mighty need surging within Mr Vane-Hovell-Vane.

'Is my daughter here?' he asked politely.

There was a long silence. Then Pearl said quietly: 'I'm very sorry to tell you she passed away.'

Edward Vane-Hovell-Vane fell to his knees on the wet planks. He held his face in his hands, as if his face were his loved child, and his body shook soundlessly.

Things were going badly for Pearl.

In fact, Mr and Mrs Edward Vane-Hovell-Vane were major donors to the school. They had endowed the science block, or, as it was known, the VHV Block. Mrs Vane-Hovell-Vane had attended the school thirty years earlier. How well I recall my mother telling me: 'The Vane-Hovell-Vanes are coming. Say something about her hat.'

Edward Vane-Hovell-Vane took some time in front of the three graves: those of his daughter, my mother and Barbara Pulmow.

After this he was conducted into the refectory, where he was served cocoa. He drank this solemnly. He refused a meal, though he must have been hungry. Then he was taken through the classrooms to the assembly hall. This route was rather important for what happened next.

A seat was prepared for him on stage, next to Pearl and the three captains: Robyn Loss-Stevenson, wearing an ochre cloak with a hood; Mary-Dot Golding, who had cut off all her hair; and Amber Wells, sporting spherical filigree earrings in red-gold, formerly the property of Miss Guss. Pearl herself wore nothing more elaborate than her own school uniform, which she had preserved in excellent condition.

'How have you survived here?' Mr Vane-Hovell-Vane asked, having quickly adjusted to the fact that the shrunken vestige of a girl known as Pearl was, in fact, the person to whom comments should be addressed.

'We've been very lucky,' Pearl said. 'We had supplies. And the island is home to a lot of seabirds.'

'Ah,' said Mr Vane-Hovell-Vane. 'You're hunting them, are you?' He glanced, perhaps a little warily, at the audience.

'Yes,' said Pearl.

'What about water?'

'We dug a well,' said Pearl.

'Remarkable,' said Mr Vane-Hovell-Vane. 'Remarkable. And there are no adults here?'

'No.'

'What happened to the teachers?'

'They were away on the mainland at the time.'

He sighed. 'Terrible business. And you've had a visitor, you say.'

'Yes.'

'What happened to him?' asked Mr Vane-Hovell-Vane.

There was a pause. 'We're quite willing,' said Pearl at length, 'to answer any questions you might have. But I hope you won't mind if we ask some of our own. For example, the

G.W. Dexter

scope of the war. Was it confined to Britain? Or Britain and Europe? What about the Far East?'

Mr Vane-Hovell-Vane was prepared to indulge her. 'I'm afraid it's impossible to say. There are rumours. Nothing definite. The Continent was certainly affected. It's possible the war was limited to Europe, but if that were the case, we'd have seen something from our American friends. I haven't seen a single plane in the air for nearly a year. It seems likely that America was affected in much the same way as we are here. That would argue that our Allies in the East, Japan, Singapore, India, were also affected. But as I say, there's very little evidence.'

Pearl turned to the student body. 'Does the school have any questions?' she said.

'What about London?' asked someone.

'London appears to have been hit pretty hard, I'm afraid.'

'Sheffield?'

With the mention of this unlikely city, Mr Vane-Hovell-Vane seemed belatedly to realise that the question was not about the locale *per se*, but the denizens therein, and thus was equivalent to asking: 'Are my parents dead?'

He made a transparent attempt to lie. 'Sheffield may have survived,' he said.

'Camberley?'

'Camberley. Well, Camberley is to the west of London, isn't it. Well outside the... the area.'

'Scarborough?'

'It's... it's difficult to say of course, but Scarborough is... considerably... I imagine there is a good possibility it escaped.'

It was becoming increasingly obvious that Mr Vane-Hovell-Vane had made his way to the coast through a wasteland of glowing rubble.

'And you're in Bristol, is that correct?' asked Pearl.

'Yes.'

'And was Bristol…'

Mr Vane-Hovell-Vane muttered something.

'And Mrs Vane-Hovell-Vane?'

'My wife is dead.'

'I'm very sorry to hear that. How did it happen that you survived?'

Mr Vane-Hovell-Vane hesitated momentarily. 'Well. I was in the cellar. The bomb went off… She was upstairs. The house collapsed on top of her. On top of me. It took me four days to dig my way out.'

'Was there a warning, then?' asked Pearl. 'About the nuclear strike? A siren?'

'No,' said Mr Vane-Hovell-Vane in mildly mystified tones. 'No warning.'

'Then why were you in the cellar?' asked Pearl.

It struck me that this was the cleverest question I had ever heard Pearl ask. Because there is rarely any entirely virtuous reason for being alone in a cellar.

Mr Vane-Hovell-Vane gulped. 'I have… I *had*… a model train set,' he said. He stopped, perhaps wondering whether to make a joke of it, then rushed on irrelevantly. 'Everyone was dead, you see. We… the survivors… formed a sort of community. We tried to find food. There were other communities.'

'And you fought them,' said Pearl.

'Yes,' said Mr Vane-Hovell-Vane absently. Something had taken his attention. He was staring out of the window. He raised a quivering finger. 'What is *that*?' he asked.

The assembly hall's windows were boarded up on the west side. On the east, the windows were undamaged. Just outside the east wall was the cage of the beast-man. The beast-man had been asleep in his tent, but had chosen that moment to put out his matted head, perhaps in expectation of food.

Pearl did not reply.

Mr Vane-Hovell-Vane got to his feet, still pointing out of the window. 'Who is that?' he asked. He began to descend the little wooden steps at the side of the stage. Pearl and the three captains, as well as the rest of the school, followed him out of the double doors on the south side, into the lobby and out onto the side-lawn near the quad. There Mr Vane-Hovell-Vane stopped in front of the beast-man's cage.

'Who is this?' he asked for the third time, fine strands of his hair flying about his ears. He indicated the beast-man, who had scrambled to his feet. Mr Vane-Hovell-Vane glared at Pearl. 'I insist that you answer me.'

'This man,' said Pearl steadily, 'attempted to rape one of the girls.'

'Attempted?'

'Yes, attempted.'

'Did he succeed?'

'It was mouth rape,' said Alana March.

Mr Vane-Hovell-Vane walked up to the bars. 'Who are you?' he asked.

The beast-man cleared his throat. 'My name is Fisher Kington,' he croaked.

'Why are you here?' asked Mr Vane-Hovell-Vane.

'I came... for food,' the beast-man said. 'But they... they hit me over the head and tied me up. Then they locked me in here. They shot me with arrows. I helped them build that wall. You better go – they'll do it to you too.'

Mr Vane-Hovell-Vane stood in a daze. Then he turned round to face us. He raised his chin again. He strode the few paces towards Pearl. 'Right, little miss,' he said. 'This is ridiculous. You can't keep him in there in those conditions.

The man's skin and bone. Look at him, he's filthy. How long has he been like that?'

'About eleven months,' said Pearl.

'Through the winter?' he asked, incredulous.

'We supplied him with a tent and blankets.'

'Really. This is inhumane. Really. I would've thought you'd know better. This is a fee-paying school. I insist that you release him or at least find him an alternative place to live. Let him have a bath. He's probably lousy. Give me the key.'

Pearl nodded to herself. 'You are an honourable man, Edward. But you are misguided. We will do as we think fit. His imprisonment is a decree of the school council.'

'Who has the key here?' asked Mr Vane-Hovell-Vane loudly. 'Who has the key?'

'Me,' said Bettina Farque in a small voice.

'Please give it to me,' said Mr Vane-Hovell-Vane in tones that retained traces of the world-weary disciplinarian he had once, no doubt, been. He walked toward Bettina and stood towering over her. He held his hand out. 'Give it to me.'

Bettina made no move to comply.

'Did you hear what I said?' asked Mr Vane-Hovell-Vane. 'I want you to GIVE ME THE KEY.'

And with that he grabbed Bettina's wrist.

Pearl made a movement with her hand and Fritzi raised her bow and shot him dead.

We buried him next to his daughter.

So now we had two boats: a sailboat and a row-boat. Our collection of boats was growing as fast as our collection of graves.

A debate on the killing of Edward Vane-Hovell-Vane was held on the 10th April 1976, shortly before the anniversary of the end of the world on the 25th. The resolution was: 'This house believes that the killing of Edward Vane-Hovell-Vane was unjustified.' Proposing the resolution were Laura Huxley and Hillary Kaplan; opposing it were Tom Keck and Alice Celia Swash.

The debate was poorly attended. Most felt that, given the fact that Edward Vane-Hovell-Vane was under several feet of soil, there was nothing in particular to argue about. And in the event, more than four-fifths of the vote went against the resolution. Tom Keck's summary rebuttal was particularly powerful, asserting that if Mr Vane-Hovell-Vane had taken the key from Bettina, and had subsequently released the beast-man, Mr Vane-Hovell-Vane and the beast-man would have been in charge of the school; the beast-man would then have exacted his promised revenge, and what Mr Vane-Hovell-Vane would have done was an unknown quantity. It's hard to predict the behaviour of a man who plays with model train sets.

Laura Huxley was thus dealt another defeat.

Laura's coterie, as I have said, included Beulah Gaze, who, by this time, had become entirely converted to blubber; Paula Ott, formerly the fattest girl in the school, who had slimmed down remarkably; and Pamela Gowler, who had phobias about mice and sleeping. Its other members included Lisa Plast, whose main ambition was to drive a car wearing gloves; and Camilla Moon Khan, who doubted everything anyone said. The main connection between the six girls was that in the past their families had been able to afford to spend parts of the year in places that were either hotter or cooler, as demanded, than the places that everyone else could afford to go to. Now, of course, things were rather different, including temperatures.

Laura's coterie did not actually refuse to abide by the decisions of the council, but they did keep up a background grumbling.

I had known Laura reasonably well for several years. I think the fact that I was the headmistress's son gave me a certain lustre. Though, as I have said, we didn't personally get along. So it was with some surprise that I looked up from my plate one lunchtime and saw Laura standing over me with a tray.

'Mind if I join you?' she asked.

'Go ahead.'

She sat down. Immediately the conversation turned to Pearl.

'You see,' she said, 'the problem isn't so much what Pearl's doing now. It's what she'll be doing in a year's time. If we let her.'

'How do you mean?'

'She's getting more and more above herself. We don't have debates any more.'

'We just had one.'

'Not as many.' She lifted a forkful of puffin to her mouth. 'The council decide everything.'

'We can't have debates on every little thing.'

She laughed, lowering her untasted puffin. 'Really, Stephen. I would have thought that you, above all, would see our point.'

Titty had said exactly the same thing.

'Who,' Laura continued, 'do you think is on the council? Amber, Mary-Dot and Robyn. Brown-nosing her all the time.'

This was so revolting an image that I wondered if I'd heard her correctly. 'What is it that you and the others actually want?' I said.

'We've drawn up four principles.'

I found my interest piqued. 'What?'

Laura finished her mouthful. 'First, we are pro-relations with men, in free and equal partnerships. Second, we are pro-childbearing. Third, we are pro-expansionist. And fourth, we are pro-civilisation. We are pro-reconstruction of society. Places with proper electricity. Proper… museums and films and stuff.'

'Well, I like museums.'

'Pearl is a reactionary. But somehow she manages to make everyone do what she says. She's even got *you* eating out of your hand.'

'Don't you mean eating out of *her* hand?'

'That's what I said,' Laura said. (The reader can check this.) 'Which is pretty funny, given that she thinks you're basically the beast-man's younger brother.'

'That's just Pearl,' I said.

'Don't be too sure. She's capable of killing someone in cold blood to get what she wants. We saw that. You'd better tread carefully.'

She was, in her way, right. Pearl was ruthless. Or was she simply clear-sighted?

'If you want to change who's on the council,' I said, 'run for election. You could start by running against Francesca.'

'Oh yes, of course, brilliant idea,' Laura said. 'Free paperclips for everyone.'

'You don't think you'd get the votes?'

'It's a waste of time. Deputies don't have any power. To get on the council I'd have to run against Mary-Dot. They all love her. No one's forgotten her telling the beast-man off. And she's always going on about getting drunk and having sex.'

'Well that's what you want, isn't it?'

Laura threw me a withering glance. 'No, it isn't,' she said. 'The four principles are about marriage, not about having it off. It's a completely different thing.'

'Well, you've got Paula. Paula supports you, doesn't she?'

'Yes.'

'Get her to take over from Robyn.'

'That twit? Pearl would never let it happen.'

'Well, in that case, your options are a bit limited.'

'Not necessarily. That's what I'm saying. We don't have to do what Pearl says all the time. We're free agents. Why can't we make a trip to the mainland? Just to see with our own eyes what on earth is going on over there? We've got a sailboat now.'

'Do you know how to sail?'

'God, what a defeatist! We could learn! Isn't this place getting you down? Aren't you curious?'

'All right,' I said slowly – it is always wise to speak slowly in a school bristling with bows and arrows – 'I can see what you're saying. But you could at least wait until the wall is finished. Then you can do what you like and start making contact and so on and no one will get hurt.'

Laura stared at me. 'My God, listen to you!' she cried. 'You opposed the wall! Remember?' She collected her cups and plates and stood up, bobbed hair swinging. 'I knew your heart wasn't in it. That's why we lost. The wall is a waste of time. If we don't try to make contact we're all doomed. I would have thought that would be obvious even to you.' She held her tray out as if she were about to tip it over me. 'Instead of going on about men we need to work out ways we can live with them.'

And with a little cry of exasperation she turned on her heel and went to sit somewhere else.

By late March work on the wall had resumed.

It was a mild March. In fact, winter as a whole had been mild. It had snowed, but it hadn't settled much. Likewise, at the height of the previous summer, things had never got much above warmish. It seemed that the effect of the war was to eliminate the climate.

In early April, Pearl called me into her office in the Lodge.

'I want you to help me with something,' she said. 'We have open views to the coast in the direction of the mainland. But we can't see anything to the east.'

'True. Unless we go up there.'

'Yes, but even then, the view is restricted, isn't it? The north and south are blocked off too. What I want is to build something that will give us an all-round view of the island. A watchtower. Maybe about thirty feet high. I've asked Bettina as well. I want you to help her.'

'Oh,' I said. Another Pearl vanity project.

Pearl startled me by banging on the desk with the flat of her hand. 'Come on!' she cried. 'I need you! You're a thinker. You've got more brain-cells than most of the rest of them put together. But you don't seem to make much use of them. Apart from lying on your bed reading Dostoevsky.'

'I've just had a whole afternoon of Forti 3,' I said, with a touch of hauteur.

'That's not much of a stretch for you,' she said. 'You're a boy. You're stronger than the rest. Come on, I want you to shape up.' She stared at me. 'What would your mother say?'

I began to feel seriously annoyed. 'Who knows? She's dead.'

Pearl seemed to realise she had gone too far. 'Yes. All right. Look, Stephen, I don't want you to build it yourself. I want you to *think* about it. Think, think.' She tapped the side of her head. 'We need people who are thinkers. Planners. Who can look a year ahead, five years ahead, ten years ahead. Do you expect me to do it all?' She glanced at me slyly. 'Do you want me to be the tyrant of Near?'

Was Pearl bugging the refectory?

I considered the ceiling. 'No. But not everyone's as intense as you are.'

'Well, they should be,' said Pearl, getting up from her chair.

She really was extraordinarily small. And she would be sixteen soon. Perhaps she was sixteen already. Perhaps she was thirty. It was really impossible to tell.

She walked round the desk and stood in front of me, tapping a six-inch ruler into her palm.

'I know I'm not strong, Stephen,' she said. 'I know I'm not much of anything. But I do have the interests of this school at heart.' She smiled. 'How tall are you now?'

'I don't know,' I said.

'Let me measure you. Stand against the wall. Over there.'

'Why?'

'Please.'

I walked over to the wall near the window and stood with my hands at my sides. Pearl crouched down by the skirting-board and rested the end of the rule on the floor. I felt her mousy hair brush my shins. Then, marking carefully with a pencil, she made her way up the wall to my shoulders. Standing on tiptoe, she marked the wall above my head.

'Five feet and nine inches,' she said. You're taller than anyone in the school except for Anne Heaviside.'

'Have you measured her as well?'

Pearl put the ruler on the desk. 'No,' she said. 'That would be a little insensitive, don't you think?'

I didn't say anything.

'Stephen, I am not a tyrant, and I am not a madwoman.'

'I know.'

'But I need your help. I want that tower. Think about it.'

My mother. Ardent solver of crossword puzzles. *The Telegraph* in twenty minutes.

'Stephen! How many types of bat do you know?'

'Pipistrelle, fruit bat, vampire bat. Cricket bat.'

'Ah! Cricket bat! Clever boy! Thank you!' Head down. 'All right, five across. Seven letters, third letter 'c'. "Half-nude, see-through sort of family." Ah. Nu-clear. Nuclear.'

It all seems so long ago. Now we are all orphans. Titty is an orphan. Alison Barclay-Coutts is an orphan. Camilla Moon Khan is probably an orphan. Even Yolanda Vane-Hovell-Vane, orphaned in death. An orphan can't complain about his lot in front of fifty-four other orphans (fifty-three, minus Barbara Pulmow). In the Black Hole of Calcutta, comments about the cramped conditions were generally deprecated.

And of course Pearl is also an orphan. Head Orphan.

I remember my mother looking with interest on the fourteen-year-old Pearl. Pearl was captain of Darling, after all. A girl with a future. Head Girl material. Perhaps a leader of men. I think my mother had plans for Pearl.

But what does Pearl know, what does she really know, of what my mother would have wanted for her only son?

Pamela Gowler knew about it; so did Camilla Moon Khan. But they hadn't been brave enough. The first anyone else knew about it was when Emma-Jane Crotch saw a sail on the horizon.

'It's another one!' she screamed.

Only it wasn't another one. It was Laura Huxley, out in the open ocean, having stolen the sailboat.

We rushed down to the jetty.

I suppose Laura was about three hundred yards out, or the distance a PG Wodehouse hero can drive a golf ball.

Robyn Loss-Stevenson came running down to the shore. '*The Puffin Book of Sailing* is missing from the library!' she panted.

'Well, she's making good use of it,' Pearl said equably.

Edward Vane-Hovell-Vane's boat was a small craft with one sail. There was a light breeze from the east. If the wind kept up, it would blow her to the mainland. Would she come back, loaded down with electricity, medicines and husbands?

At three hundred yards we could see her strategy quite clearly: the boom was secured at one side with a rope, and Laura was perching on the other to keep the boat level. Her course was true and steady. Three hundred yards became three hundred and fifty. One couldn't help but admire her pluck.

More girls joined us. Someone brought some binoculars from the Lodge, and we took turns with them. We waved, though Laura, intent on the pinkish landmass to the west, did not seem to see us.

And then suddenly the sail disappeared.

Cries went up.

Deedee Foe had the binoculars. 'Can you see?' I said.

'Wait… she's… she's gone over,' said Deedee.

'May I?' I asked, taking the instrument.

I looked. The sailboat was lying in the light swell. The hull floated on its side, a small fin sticking out. The sail itself clung to the surface of the water, as responsive as litter. And clinging to the fin was Laura Huxley, her hair sleek over her face. And no life-jacket.

Pearl took the binoculars. She looked for a while without comment, then handed them to Mary-Dot.

'We've got to help her!' cried Zillah Smith. 'We can't leave her there!'

Pearl said nothing.

'Come on, Stephen!' Zillah cried again.

'What?' I said.

'Come on!' said Zillah. She pointed to the row-boat. 'Get in! One oar each.'

I looked at Pearl. She nodded.

High in the midsummer heavens, two clouds momentarily parted and a shard of azure sky appeared, the shape of an uneven grin. No sun was visible, but just under the shard was a sunlit cumulus.

'Blue!' screamed Eufemia Paleocapa.

The clouds closed up again. Titty hadn't seen it. Where was she? Almost the whole school was on the beach by now. Amber Wells, Polly Findhorn, Camilla Moon Khan, Bee Wasket, Helen Maitland, Henry Keck, Alana March, Julia Fitt-Matt, Beulah Gaze, Samara Slavens, Bettina Farque, Eunice Riddley, and thirty or so others… but no Titty.

I jumped into the rowboat beside Zillah. We began to pull hard toward Laura. We were evenly matched. Zillah's grunts were comfortingly familial.

The seas were placid, but it was hard work. It took a full twenty minutes to arrive at the idly-drifting boat and its idly-drifting pilot. We manoeuvred the rowboat around to Laura. Her lips were blue and her face white. Her eyes were unfocussed and her head was trembling. But she was alive.

Zillah leant far out on one side while I leant over the other to prise Laura's fingers off the fin. Then I put my arms around her, dragged her over the side of the row-boat and slither-dumped her in the bottom. She lay there curled and shivering.

'Give her your coat!' cried Zillah. 'She's going to freeze to death.'

I took off my coat and wrapped it round her.

'Here,' said Zillah,' handing me a leather jacket filched from the wardrobe of Miss Steel. 'Put that over her too.'

We struck out for Near. My main concern was whether Titty would, by now, have joined the watchers at the beach.

I was surprised to see Zillah stop rowing. 'What about the sailboat?' she asked. 'Can we tow it?'

'Don't be silly,' I said. 'We've got to get her back fast.'

'But don't you think Pearl will want it?'

'Balls to Pearl,' I said.

Zillah looked at the half-drowned Laura. 'All right.'

We pulled hard for the shore and in another twenty minutes had beached up. Laura was carried into the school.

Pearl, ignoring the shivering Laura, was still holding the binoculars. 'Let's monitor it,' she said slowly. 'I think it's drifting this way.'

And in fact the boat was perceptibly closer than when we'd started out.

'It's going to come in,' said Pearl finally. 'If you wouldn't mind, just wait until you can get to it easily and then bring it back.'

And with that she walked off back to the school.

Titty was still nowhere to be seen.

Later that same day I went to the art room and found a brush and some black paint. I took some rolls of old wallpaper I'd found in a cupboard in the Shute Building, and cut them into poster-sized lengths. These I spread out on the floor of my bedroom.

On the back of the first I wrote, in capitals eight inches high: 'She is fat.'

On the second I wrote: 'She is ugly.'

On the third: 'She is boring.'

On the fourth: 'She is stupid.'

On the fifth: 'She is passionless.'

These I put up on my walls with drawing-pins. Then I lay down on the floor and looked at them, reading them over and over again. A slow sickness stirred in my guts. I ran to the wastepaper bin. I retched. I slumped.

Tears came.

Bettina Farque loved horses and dogs. There were unfortunately no dogs on the island.

Bettina was a stocky girl with blonde hair tied up behind. She had a wide, plain face that seemed to hide nothing. Looking at her, one felt one's own face relax.

Bettina spent most of her time in the workshop, excused from lessons. Apart from Pearl, she was probably the most useful person on the island.

I found her there, sharpening a plane with a file. We only had one plane, and it got a lot of use.

'Pearl sent me,' I said. 'She wants to build a watchtower.'

'Yes, she told me,' said Bettina, continuing to sharpen.

'I had a thought,' I said. 'Maybe we don't have to build it, as such. We could just make a treehouse.'

Bettina continued sharpening. 'There's not really enough room at the top of a pine tree, is there? I mean, the branches don't spread out enough.'

'Yes,' I said, 'but you wouldn't build it in just one tree. You'd build it in three or four trees.'

Bettina stopped sharpening, straightened up and rubbed her neck.

'Here,' I said. 'I'll draw it.' I got out a notebook and sketched three trees standing close together. I joined up the top of each tree to make a triangle. 'You put planks on top, here, to make a base,' I said, sketching in the requisite members. 'Then you put a rail round the side, to stop people falling off. You could even have a roof. Actually you'd probably need one if you wanted people to go up there in bad weather.'

'Are there any trees in the right place?' asked Bettina. 'That close together?'

'I've found a few that might work. Right up on the ridge. At the top. They got burned but they're still alive. They're alive inside. And they're exactly where we need them.'

'Wouldn't we need to be up higher than the other trees?'

'Not if we're at the highest point of the ridge.'

Bettina went back to her sharpening.

'If we still couldn't see,' I went on, 'we could fell some of the trees around them. It would be easier than burying new poles in the ground.'

'How would we get up there?'

'Ladder.'

Bettina blew on the sharpened blade. 'Not a bad idea,' she said finally. 'I'll go up tomorrow and take a look.'

'Okay. I'll come with you.'

Such was my conversation with Bettina Farque.

As I have said, I lived somewhat apart from the girls. I had two rooms: a study room and a bedroom. The girls lived cheek by jowl in the dorms.

No one ever visited me. Occasionally, Robyn, as house captain, might put a note under my door if the matter were urgent. Otherwise I might find a memo in my pigeonhole.

It was surprising, therefore, to hear a knock on my study-room door one afternoon after school. Opening said portal, I beheld Fritzi Pietsch from Hamm (or Fritzi Hamm from Pietsch). She was still wearing her fetching little rabbit-fur cap. It must have been pinned on.

'Hello,' she said, smiling.

I don't know why, but I had the impression she was not alone, that someone else was hiding, though I couldn't see or hear anyone.

She was holding something. 'We made this for you,' she said.

It was a small object wrapped in tinfoil. 'What is it?' I asked.

'A cake,' she said. 'We baked it. Without sugar. It's more like bread, really. But it's got cinnamon in it. And guillemot eggs.'

'Thank you.'

'We wanted to thank you for saving Laura.'

I should say that Fritzi's voice had a rather charming Germanic cadence. 'Thank' came out more like 'sank'.

'Oh, that's all right,' I said. 'It was Zillah, really.'

'No!' she cried, as if offended. 'It was you.' (*It vos you.*)

'All right,' I said. 'It was me.'

Fritzi peered past me. 'Aren't you going to invite me in?'

I looked behind me at the study room. Dirty plates and cups lay strewn on the floor. Books and papers rose in tottering stacks. The window was covered by a grubby bedspread. Since Albert had left I hadn't made much of an effort. The windows were closed and the room was musty; I couldn't myself smell anything, but I knew the smell was there. Fritzi, however, didn't seem to notice.

I stepped back to allow her to enter.

'Nice big room,' she said, walking in. She stopped by my desk. 'Are you still studying?'

'No.'

'What's this then?' she asked, picking up a primer on Japanese grammar.

'It's Japanese,' I said. 'Just for fun.'

She raised a Teutonic eyebrow. 'How can learning Japanese be fun?'

I shrugged.

'That was a very brave thing you did,' said Fritzi, returning to the subject. 'And getting the sailboat back. That was clever. We might need that.'

'It sort of came back by itself.'

'What do you do in here all on your own?' she said, abandoning it. 'You should learn German.'

'I am learning German. At least, I was learning German.'

'Shall we speak German?'

'I've forgotten most of it,' I said.

'Well, it's an ugly language.'

'I like it.'

'Really? Oh, that's nice of you. Most people seem to think it's ugly. I suppose it's because we lost the war. What's in here?'

'My bedroom.'

'Can I look?'

I felt a surge of horror. The posters were still up. 'It's private,' I said.

'If you say so.' Fritzi wandered over to the window. She looked down. Her gaze rested on the beast-man's cage, about fifty yards away. 'Do you think it was wrong, what I did to the beast-man?'

'I don't know. Would you do it again?'

She pondered. 'He seems to have healed up.'

'That can't be the only consideration,' I said.

'Well, what would you have done?'

'I don't know.'

'Don't keep saying "I don't know" all the time. It's not very attractive.' Fritzi looked down on Ludivine Nockolds, sitting on silent guard duty outside the ten-foot circle. 'Do you think Ludivine's pretty?'

I moved a little closer to her vantage-point. 'Yes,' I said. 'Or no.'

'What do you mean?' asked Fritzi, in annoyed tones. 'Which one, yes or no?'

'She's quite...' I said, struggling for an adjective.

'Quite what?'

'Quite pretty.'

Fritzi looked up at me critically. 'Don't you think about girls, Stephen?' she said.

I met her eyes with difficulty. There were five freckles on her face, positioned on her left eyebrow, left cheek, nose, right cheek and lower right cheek. She was astonishingly lovely. I looked away.

'I can't not think about them,' I said, 'living here.'

Fritzi pursed her lips. 'Well, that's a start. Who do you like best, then? I mean, on the island.'

'Murray Mint,' I said.

'That would be funny,' said Fritzi austerely, 'if Murray Mint were female. Come on, I want your opinion. People want to know who it is.'

'What people?'

'What people do you think? Of course, I've got my own theory about who you like.'

Titty, Titty, Titty. I began to panic. 'Well, Rowena is very attractive,' I said, picking the least appealing girl I could think of, then wishing I hadn't.

'That's just cruel,' said Fritzi. 'Rowena is a very nice person.'

'All right. Sorry. Please don't tell her I said that. She's a bit annoying, but I'm sure she's very nice. I didn't mean to make fun of her.'

Fritzi regarded me coolly. 'You're very serious, aren't you?' Without moving away from me, or even taking her eyes from mine, she picked up another book from a pile on top of a chair. 'What's this one?'

Horror stole over me once more. It was *Justine*, by the Marquis de Sade. I'd found it in the effects of Miss Swift, who taught geography and domestic science.

'It's a book about France,' I said.

'Oh,' said Fritzi. 'Well, that's dull.' She hefted the book experimentally in one hand. 'I think I should tell you what I'm really here for.'

'Oh.'

'We wondered when you are going to do something.'

I am not stupid.

'Do what?' I asked stupidly.

'Do whatever you want to.'

My mind had rusted shut. I felt like throwing myself out of the window, or hitting her. I think I would have been glad to have seen her dead.

'No, it's okay,' I said. 'I'm not really... I'm not really interested.'

Fritzi considered me stonily. 'You're the only boy on the island.'

'Yes,' I said. 'But...' I shrugged and smiled, as if it were a joke.

Fritzi let *Justine* fall from her fingers onto the pile. Whatever good there had been between us, whatever element of charm or connection, whatever harmless flirtation, drained away as if it had never been there. I felt like crying. I knew what it was to be rejected. Now I had rejected her.

She moved away from the window and towards the door. On the way there, as if on an impulse, she grabbed the door handle of my bedroom and flung the door wide.

Her face blossomed with delight.

'Who is?' she asked.

'What?'

'Ugly?'

'You are!' I said without thinking.

Fritzi came closer. She stood under me menacingly. 'I'm not ugly, Stephen. And I'm not –' she checked through the open door – 'passionless. And I'm not fat. Or boring.'

I didn't say anything.

'So…' Fritzi said. 'Who are you in love with?'

'I'm not in love with anyone.'

'Of course you are,' she said. 'Who is it?'

On an impulse, I grabbed her. I kissed her. Our teeth clashed. She gave a small cry, but she didn't resist. Then I pushed her away. We stood apart, breathing heavily. It wasn't really a kiss at all. It was an attempt to shut her up. There was no desire. It was as if I'd slapped her or called her a name.

We looked at each other for a long time, stunned. Then she turned.

'Don't tell anyone!' I said.

Fritzi left the room.

I ran out and caught up with her as she was about to descend the stairs. 'Are… are you…' I stuttered. 'Are you Fritzi Pietsch from Hamm or Fritzi Hamm from Pietsch?'

She turned. 'Peach?' There was not the smallest hint of amusement on her exquisite face. 'I'm from Merzig. And my last name is Peitz.'

Fritzi Merzig. From Peitz. Where on earth had I got the idea that she was Fritzi Pietsch? Or Fritzi Hamm? Merzig did not sound anything like Pietsch, or indeed Hamm. Of course, Peitz did sound a little like Pietsch (though not like Hamm). Perhaps that was why I had allowed myself such a foolish, and yet, at the same time, such a strange, error. I had known Fritzi at least six years.

Wait, though… could it have been that during this time her family circumstances had changed, and that her new name was Hamm? Or rather, not, of course, Hamm, but Merzig? But then, even if that were the case, her place of birth could not conceivably have changed. It must always have been Peitz.

So she was Fritzi Merzig, from Peitz. I had to remember that. Fritzi Merzig, from Peitz.

Though… wait a minute… wasn't it the other way around? Wasn't she in fact Fritzi Peitz, from Merzig?

Minna Bye had spent the last nine months in the Lodge. She had done very little except learn to play the violin. When work resumed on the wall in the spring of 1976, Minna was too weak to be of much use. But every day, we heard her practising. She seemed to be getting quite good.

How do you get to Carnegie Hall? Well, these days it involves an arduous journey by rowboat.

Minna had short black hair and large black eyes. Formerly her eyes had sparkled with malice. She had always been ready with a joke or put-down, but these jokes and put-downs were usually second-hand, and not very funny.

Now Minna's eyes had changed. They were calm and intense. On the rare occasions that she spoke, she looked into your eyes, burning.

Minna's sixteenth birthday was in May. To celebrate the occasion, she announced that she would be giving a concert.

Most of the girls took an interest in music. Minna's programme was ambitious, consisting of pieces by Handel, Biber and Zelenka; the latter two, as I found out from the programme, being baroque composers of the seventeenth and eighteenth centuries.

The girls were curious, I think, about Minna.

On the evening of the concert, Minna strode onto the stage dressed in an orange skirt and brown jumper. The colours of Brownstone were very fashionable.

The Handel – *Lascio ch'io pianga*, a sad tune – was met with enthusiastic applause. Titty, in the front row, was the most enthusiastic of all.

The Biber, which, according to the programme, was from his *Sonata representativa*, consisting of short pieces representing birds and animals, was received with cheers.

The Zelenka was a little dismal, but one can't have everything.

Minna then performed her own composition, which she called 'Tree felling'. It seemed to draw on the Biber for quirky expressiveness. The violin replicated the sound of the saw, the asthmatic in-out in-out of the blade as it bit into the trunk, the creaking as the tree began to topple, the shattering of the small branches against the other forest trees, the earth-thump of its trunk, the death-quiver of its needles, birds in panicked flight. The girls clapped and cheered.

'Tree felling' was a joke, finally, that Minna had heard from no one else.

Have you ever lain awake at night listening to someone talking? I have. In my case, it was the beast-man.

This was not unusual. As I have mentioned, my rooms were right next to the beast-man's cage, and he tended to mumble to himself. But on this occasion he seemed to be having a conversation. If I listened carefully, I thought I could hear another voice.

I walked to the window and opened it a fraction. It was too dark to see, but straining on the wind, there was, indeed, another person. A higher-pitched voice. A girl. Someone was talking to him. This was strictly forbidden.

I put on a coat, went down the stairs and out into the portico. The night was starless and moonless. I hid behind a pillar. Now I had a better view.

It was Alison Barclay-Coutts, the girl named after two banks.

She sat outside the circle. I was about ten feet away from her. I could hear the conversation quite clearly.

'I've been in love plenty of times,' the beast-man was saying. 'When I was younger.'

'Did they love you back?' asked Alison.

'Sometimes,' said the beast-man. 'But most of the time they didn't. Most of the time I didn't tell them. I was too shy.'

This was precisely the side of the beast-man that was most deleterious to harmony on the island.

'Tell me about the last time you were in love,' Alison said.

'The last time?' said the beast-man. 'Now. Now. I'm in love with you.'

'You can't be,' said Alison.

'Why not?'

'You don't know me.'

'It doesn't matter. You don't have to know someone to be in love with them. Did you always know whoever you were in love with?'

'I don't know.'

'Don't keep saying "I don't know" all the time, girl.'

'Why?'

'It might put me off you.'

I felt a bizarre envy as I heard Alison laugh.

'I don't believe you, anyway,' she said.

'Well, it doesn't matter. I am in love with you, though. Because you talked to me. I was going crazy in here. Because of that little girl. What do you call her?'

'Alice.'

'No, not Alice. The tiny one.'

'Pearl.'

'Is that her name?'

'She just wants what's best for us. She wants to protect us from… from harm.'

There was a silence.

'I am sorry, though,' said the beast-man. 'I am.'

'I hope so.'

'And I'm sorry about the bad things I said.'

'You should be.'

'And what about the boy?'

I felt myself stiffen all over.

'Who?' asked Alison.

'The boy.'

'Oh. Stephen.'

'He's sitting pretty, isn't he?'

'I don't know. Is he? I mean, I don't think he sees it like that.'

'Why not?'

'I don't know.'

'There you go again.'

'Sorry.'

'You've got to have more confidence in your own opinion.'

'All right.'

There was a pause.

'This is a right old pickle.'

'Yes.'

'This is a right old pickle, this is.'

'Yes.'

'What about Pearl? Do you think she can be talked round?'

'I don't know.'

'Don't know! One point off.'

'Sorry. I mean... maybe in the future. Not now. Maybe things will change.'

Pause.

'I ran a shop, did I tell you that?'

'No. Really?'

'Yeah.'

'Oh.'

'It's funny thinking back on it. Now look at me.'

'Things can change.'

'I hope so.'

Sickened, I crept away. Like many people, I have an aversion to hearing myself talked about.

In fact, when it came to it, I was violently against the idea of the beast-man talking to anybody.

I found Pearl by the fortifications at lunch. It was a windless day with a misty rain. She was sitting on a plastic sheet on the ground, eating a boiled gull's egg.

'Can I have a word?'

'Go ahead.'

I squatted uncomfortably on my heels. 'What's the policy on talking to the beast-man?'

'You know what it is.'

'Just tell me again – why is it that we can't talk to him?'

'Because he doesn't deserve to be talked to,' said Pearl.

'But that's not the real reason, is it?' I said.

Pearl chewed, not looking at me. 'Tell me what you think the real reason is.'

'You can't have anyone speaking to him because otherwise they'll see he's a human being, and men aren't human beings.'

Pearl looked up. 'Well that's nonsense. Of course men are human beings. They've got two arms, two legs, two eyes. What's this all about?'

'What would you do if you found out someone was talking to him?'

'Why?'

'I'm curious.'

'Do you mean Alison?' Pearl asked.

I nearly lost my balance. 'What?'

Pearl gave me a cool look. 'Alison.'

'You know about it?'

'Yes.'

'And that's all right, is it?'

'You forget, I'm at the Lodge.' Pearl smiled. 'I can hear everything.'

'And you don't mind?'

'Everyone knows about Alison.' She looked at me quizzically. 'Do you mean no one told you, Stephen?'

She began gathering the fragments of egg-shell into a pile on the sheet.

'So, that's all right, then, is it?' I said. 'Everything's fine?'

'No,' said Pearl slowly. 'It's not all right. I wouldn't want everyone doing it. But Alison got herself sent to Coventry, didn't she?'

'Yes.'

'He was the only person being talked to less than she was.'

Shame coursed over me.

'Everyone knows?'

'Yes.'

'Who told them?'

'I expect Alison told them herself. She doesn't have much to lose.' She put the egg-shell fragments into her pocket. 'And one good thing's come of it. They want to talk to her again.'

'Why?'

'They want to hear what the beast-man's got to say. Anyway, the wall's nearly finished. We can relax a few rules. Rules are made to be relaxed. Not broken. Relaxed.'

And with that she stood up, folded her sheet and put it away. Lunch was over.

It was hard, sometimes, to be Stephen Ballantyne.

We completed the wall on August 6th, 1976, a year and three months after the end of the world. We were all fifteen or sixteen years old.

It had taken us more than a year to accomplish what a Roman legion could do in an afternoon, but that did not detract from the achievement. There were six thousand men in a Roman legion and only fifty-four of us.

The wall ran the projected three hundred yards, with one snicket gate, for security, by the classrooms. This gave quick access to the most useful destination, the main seabird breeding-grounds to the north-west. The walkway, three feet from the top, ran all the way around on the inside, and at the four corners there were guard-boxes in which a girl could stand (but not sit). The wall, as planned, cut off the school from the chapel, sports hall, outbuildings and Lodge, and these were now half-dismantled.

Then there was the watchtower. This was completed a couple of weeks later by a small team of ten girls, jointly led by myself and Bettina Farque. It was a comparatively simple project. First, three of the highest pines were selected. Then a ladder was set against the first tree and a rope slung over one of the highest branches. This rope was taken back down to ground level and attached to Murray Mint's collar, so that he could draw up the timber we needed for the watchtower's base. These planks, once drawn up, were screwed flat into the upper branches, and proved extremely stable. A guardrail was added to prevent mishaps. The roof proved more of a challenge, but was effected using a surprising find: in the small cabin of Edward Vane-Hovell-Vane's boat was discovered (when the door was forced open) a spare sailcloth, which, when unfolded, covered an area of about nine square yards. This was raised on poles over the base.

This watchtower (as Pearl had anticipated) enabled us to see the island in its entirety, a thing never possible before in the history of Near. From our new height we had a view clear across the plantation towards Wideopen in the east; to where fulmars and puffins nested in the ledges in the north-west; over to the mainland, brooding shattered in the west; and towards the heathery tern-grounds in the south-west. It was windy up there, but invigorating: one could smell the sea and the burnt resin of the pines. From far below came the tinny cries of girls as they exhorted each other to this task or that, or inflicted minor injuries on themselves.

Of course, one could also now see the school as a whole. Formerly open and undefended, the school now bristled magnificently with spiked staves. At last, Pearl's plan had been realised. The shape of the wall was a rectangle, like a playing card.

It might as well have been a capital letter 'P'.

You might have thought that the timetable would change after the wall was finished. Well, it did. But there was still hard physical labour.

This was in order to create the exterior ditch already mentioned. This ditch (which Pearl termed the *fossa*), was eight feet wide and six feet deep, and ran, of course, all the way around the wall. The spoil from this *fossa* was piled up on both sides of the staves, forming a sloping bank four feet in height and four feet in width each side (the *agger*, in ditch-building parlance). Additional spoil was deposited in a smaller, lower bank at a distance of twenty-four feet from the wall, again circumscribing the school. This lower bank was planted with hundreds of rose-cuttings – though I never saw the undertaking come to full efflorescence. Signs were posted at intervals to warn intruders that the rose-line represented the point at which they would attract deadly fire. A competition was held to determine what should go on the signs. Among the entries were:

'The flower may delight, but the thorn punishes.' (Emma-Jane Crotch)

'Stranger, pass this rose at your peril.' (Eunice Riddley)

'Beware my thorns.' (Helen Maitland)

But the winning entry, inscribed on dozens of signs by that talented calligrapher, Samara Slavens, was:

'Keep out or we will shoot you.' (Bettina Farque)

Sometimes, as Plato tells us, those who cannot write poetry are the most qualified to produce it.

Near School for Girls had changed greatly since April 1975. The girls had gained in stature and strength. We were fitter, more confident.

From her grassy grave, I am sure that my mother, champion of girls' education, regarded developments with a benign eye.

But one may stretch irony only so far. My dear mother could not regard anything with anything.

If we were fitter, happier, or stronger, these were incongruities in a world devastated by disease, misery and death. Our island, by sheer good fortune, had not been included in the cataclysm that had burned a million babies alive and destroyed the flower of Eastern and Western civilisation.

And some of the flotsam of that cataclysm was soon to visit us.

FIVE

I saw them first. I was high up on the watchtower. It was the March of 1977.

Another mild winter had passed. The sky was still obscured by grey banks of cloud. On rare occasions, a short-lived shaft of sunlight would cascade to earth.

The island's flora and fauna were in rude health. Seabirds gathered in greater numbers than ever before. In January I saw my first lesser black-backed gull. The lesser black-backed gull is distinguishable from the black-headed gull by not having a black head, and having a black back. There is also a great black-backed gull, but I had never seen one. It is the largest of all gulls, and remained an ambition.

On Wideopen, seals basked, bickered and bred.

We were all now sixteen years old. Some, such as Pearl, were seventeen. I would be seventeen in July.

Polly Findhorn had been replaced as deputy of Wideopen by Alana March. Francesca Mond had been replaced as deputy of Mancoe by Laura Huxley. Laura had listened to my advice and gone the way of the ballot box.

Julia Fitt-Matt had ceased to be a vegetarian and had become a hunter. Jules Cashford had renounced Satanism and had invented her own religion. Bettina Farque had thrown herself into the pleasures of demolition. Bee Wasket had nearly suffocated in a rabbit-hole trying to catch rabbits. Fritzi Merzig from Peitz (or Fritzi Peitz from Merzig) was no longer the most beautiful girl in the school, though she was still very beautiful. Harriet Gupping was long and soupy; Eufemia Paleocapa had smouldering sideburns; Pamela Gowler had chiselled features and chiselled hands. Samara Slavens had taken up Chinese calligraphy. Alice Celia Swash had not mentioned dental hygiene products for almost two years. Paula Ott was now positively willowy. Minna Bye had founded a string quartet. Emma-Jane Crotch had broken a leg. Hillary Kaplan had begun writing a book, though no one knew what it was about.

Alison spent more and more time with the beast-man. The beast-man was hairier.

I myself had begun shaving, using equipment found in the personal effects of our teachers.

The only person who had not changed was Pearl. At seventeen she looked only barely different to the way she had looked at fourteen. The exception was her nose, which had grown longer and taken on the shape of some edible root. Her school uniform never seemed to get dirty, and it never needed to be altered.

But I digress.

Seven men and one woman. Seven beast-men and one beast-woman. Or perhaps she was no beast-woman but their slave and prisoner.

They arrived in a craft halfway between a tugboat and a Viking ship. It had no engine, but possessed a central sail and three oars either side. In its stern was a small cabin.

The boat beached up on our northern shore, sending birds scattering. The beast-men jumped out and, taking hold of a rope, pulled the boat up onto the strand. They then sank a stake into the ground with a hammer. They tied the boat to the stake.

This I watched with binoculars from my eyrie. Fear and excitement made the instrument tremble. Then I remembered what I was on the watchtower for. I threw myself down the ladder, ran for the school, skirted the wall's southern corner, and sprinted for the Shute Building, where I broke in on Pearl.

'It's beast-men!' I blurted out. 'Seven of them. And a woman.'

'Sound the alarm,' Pearl said to Henry.

Within five minutes the school had assembled in front of the Shute Building.

It was Pearl's first martial address. She stood on a box, looking out over the school. Her manner was firm, her countenance grim.

'I will make this brief. Men have landed on the north shore of the island. Stephen has seen them. Seven men and one woman. It's not known when they will approach the school. It's not known if they're armed. Stephen will be re-dispatched to the watchtower as soon as I have finished speaking, to monitor their movements. As soon as they approach the school we'll be informed. They know we're here. They've come because we're here. Nothing else can yet be said.

'Your duty is to the school. Your duty is to our life here. They can't take us over; we're protected. This is the moment we've prepared for all these long months. We're armed. We're ready.'

Ululations. Cheers.

'All girls will now take up their defensive positions. No girl will fire until the command is given. This is not a battle, unless they want it to be. If they fire on us, or if they approach closer than the rose-line, they will *die*.'

More howls. I had never heard Pearl say the word 'die' before. It suited her.

'The struggle for our freedom now commences. Girls, do your duty! Take up your positions!'

The girls scrambled for the walkway, bows banging on their backs. I made for the gate. But no sooner had I reached it than a shriek was heard from above.

'Beast-men!'

It was Deedee Foe on the ladder to the north-west walkway.

The beast-men must have followed the coast round, seen the school and struck inland.

I went up to join Deedee. There they were: beast-men. Pacing determinedly toward us. They were about four hundred yards off, travelling in single file. Two were armed: a young man and an older man, bringing up the rear. They all wore motley greenish or greyish coats and boots, and on their heads were close-fitting cloth hats. All had beards. The youngest seemed to be in his twenties; the next youngest in his early thirties; three further ones seemed thirtyish or fortyish; and the remaining two were unquestionably older, perhaps fifty or sixty. The sole woman was perhaps forty. She walked second in line, with an even stride. She wore long skirts and had her hair tied back. Around her waist were pouches of rabbit-skin.

The column of beast-people reached the rose-line and stopped. The *fossa* yawned before them.

The leader, an older man, held his hands up. 'We're unarmed,' he said in a pleasant baritone. He turned to the two wearing bows. 'Put down your bows,' he said.

The two men did so, slowly. So they weren't exactly armed, but then again, neither were they quite unarmed.

'Cross that line at your peril,' Pearl said. 'Please read the notice.'

They did so.

The leader pursed his lips. 'Very sensible,' he said.

'This is our school,' said Pearl. 'We do not seek violence. But we will defend our school.'

A cry rang out. It was the beast-man, shouting something in a voice made small by wind.

Everyone ignored him.

The leader spoke again. 'We're from Holy Island. To the south. I'm Cal. Pleased to meet you.'

Pearl said nothing.

'We've run out of food. Are there any teachers with you?'

'No,' said Pearl.

'I see,' said the man. Perhaps he was speculating on what usually goes wrong if children are left to run schools for themselves.

The woman stepped forward. 'I'm Philippa,' she said.

Pearl said nothing.

'We've lived on the island for two years,' said Philippa. 'Holy Island. But there's nothing left to eat. Not like here. There are no birds left. There's nothing on the mainland. We have nets, so we can catch fish. But we're getting sick. Some of us died. So we followed the coast up and came here. We don't wish you any harm.' She rummaged among her rabbit-skins. 'In fact, we brought you a present. Here.' Between her thumb and forefinger she held up a pinkish lozenge.

Our only soap had been used up about a year and a half ago. And it hadn't been pink. Philippa walked a little nearer the wall and tossed the soap up high: it landed near Pamela Gowler, who dropped it under the walkway. Two girls clambered down to retrieve it.

A younger man came forward but Philippa motioned him back with a hand. 'If we could talk,' Philippa said, 'you'd see that we wish you no harm. Can we come inside? There are things we can offer you. Information. Stores. Friendship.'

Pearl considered. For a while there was nothing but the creaking of the staves in the wind.

'All right,' she said, Pearlishly. 'We'll talk to you.' She indicated the woman. 'Just you. The others must stay in plain sight. Please move backwards and wait. I repeat, if you come nearer the wall you will be fired upon. Our bows are accurate and our arrows pierce flesh.'

Philippa sat on the stage with Pearl, much as Edward Vane-Hovell-Vane had in the spring of the previous year.

Philippa was a little older than most of our mothers. She had round eyes that seemed to retain some traces of girlishness, but her long face had fallen around the mouth. Her hair was now loose, and it fell around her shoulders, grey-brown. She sat on her chair as if she were used to waiting.

I found myself wondering whose woman she was. Or was she her own woman?

'Holy Island is near the mainland,' Pearl said. 'So why did you come here?'

The woman smiled gently. 'We tried the mainland. But there's nothing there except sickness. It was dangerous. In the cities there's radiation. And people.'

'So you thought you would come here.'

'Yes.'

'Why were you on Holy Island?'

'We were on holiday.' She paused, remembering. 'We were all strangers. Now we know one another... quite well.'

'Are there any other people there?'

'No. Some died after the war. Some left for the mainland and didn't come back. Some fell sick. Finally there was only us. We couldn't live there any longer. So we came here.'

'Do you have any fuel?'

'No.'

'Water?'

'We have a well on Holy Island. We brought some with us.'

'Are there any more boats?'

'No. They took them.'

'Who did?'

Philippa looked nervously out at the girls. 'Some people.'

'Some people,' said Pearl.

'There were arguments,' said Philippa.

'You mean fighting?'

'Yes.'

'And were any killed?'

Philippa hesitated. 'Yes,' she said.

Pearl turned to the audience of girls. 'Does anyone have any questions?'

Elizabeth Pelham put her hand on her head. 'How about children?' she asked.

'There used to be children,' said Philippa. 'Two. They were about six and four years old. They went with their parents to the mainland to find food. We don't know what happened to them.'

Zillah Smith made the customary gesture. 'Why are you going around with beast-men?'

Philippa looked surprised. 'I'm not sure they're beast-men,' she said. 'You spoke to Cal. Cal's very nice. He's a carpenter. We're Quakers. We believe in peace.'

'How old are they?' asked Laura Huxley.

Laughter.

'Laura wants their phone numbers,' said someone.

'Daniel is twenty-three,' said Philippa gently. 'He's the baby. Mark is twenty-eight. I think. Jacob and Richard are in their thirties. I think Richard might be forty. Like me. And

Keith and Michael are a bit older. I think Michael might be seventy, but he keeps it quiet. He used to be a farmer. He's very practical and very fit for his age.'

'Can he grow things?' asked Char Parr.

'We tried, but Michael says the soil isn't right. It's not fertile. It's not like here. There are so many birds here. It makes a big difference.'

'Why do birds make a difference?' asked Anne Heaviside.

'Because of their poo, cretin,' said Bee Wasket.

Laura spoke up again. 'What's Daniel's job?' she said.

Philippa looked slightly taken aback. 'I don't know,' she said. 'He doesn't really have one.'

'Oh,' said Laura.

'I mean, any more. He was at university. I can tell you about Mark. He was a teacher. He taught children. From… you know… from deprived backgrounds.'

'What's that?' asked somebody.

'People who come from families… I mean, before the war… people who came from families who weren't… very well off.'

Philippa spoke as if recalling a foreign language.

'You mean poor people?' asked Paula Ott.

'Yes,' said Philippa.

'How much more soap have you got?' asked Beulah Gaze.

'That was our last bar,' said Philippa. 'You're welcome to it.'

Laura, however, seemed unwilling to drop the matter of the former occupations of the beast-men. 'What about the others?' she said. 'What do they do?'

Philippa crinkled her face. 'Richard used to be something to do with the arts, I think. It's been a long time since we've talked about it. He had a wife in Birmingham.' She bit her lip.

'Jacob was something in the City. But I'm not sure what. He gave it up when he became a Quaker.'

'Which city?'

'London. Finance. Money, you know.'

'The beast-man said money's no good now,' said Melissa Verne.

'I promise you they're not beast-men,' Philippa said. 'They're good people, honestly. They won't hurt you. We don't want anything except peace.'

Melissa looked enquiringly at Pearl, but Pearl didn't meet her gaze.

It would be regrettable to have to kill Philippa.

'That leaves Keith,' said Laura, her eye on Pearl. A small smile flickered around Laura's mouth. 'You haven't mentioned Keith. What does Keith do?'

Titters.

'Keith is very special,' said Philippa enthusiastically. 'He used to be a policeman. He's very kind. He came to the island because he... he needed a break.'

There was a pause.

'Well,' said Pearl, ending it. 'Is that all the questions?'

Laura Huxley bounced out of her seat, hand on head. 'I don't have a question,' she said, 'but I want to say you are very welcome here. There are enough birds for everyone!' Someone, probably Pamela Gowler, started clapping, and then stopped. Laura sat down, grinning.

'Thank you, Laura,' said Pearl, who didn't seem particularly put out.

'You're welcome,' said Laura smugly.

'And thank you, Philippa,' Pearl said, turning to our guest. 'Now. I want to say something about the school. We decide everything by debate. That's why we can't give you a decision straight away. But we will have a debate tomorrow morning. In

181

the meantime, please feel free to stay on the island. We will let you know our decision tomorrow afternoon.'

Philippa was tactful enough not to intimate – in any way whatever – that Pearl was a four-foot-high girl-baby, and that it would be absurd for the policemen, farmers and carpenters encamped outside the wall to be in any way beholden to her deliberations or to those of a rabble of strangely-dressed teenaged girls. 'Thank you,' she said simply, joining her hands in a gesture as if praying.

We left the assembly hall by the side door. On the way out we passed the beast-man's cage. We could easily have left by the back entrance, but Pearl seemed particularly to wish to use the side.

Pearl stopped momentarily by the cage, much as a proud housewife, showing a visitor around, might pause before a cabinet of coronation mugs.

The beast-man stood, his beard down to his chest, chewing on something. He looked like a gnu.

'Who is that?' Philippa asked carefully.

'That is the beast-man,' said Pearl.

'I see,' said Philippa. She looked thoughtful. Then she nodded and walked on.

The beast-man, coming to his senses, made a frantic bellow, but Philippa didn't look back.

We reached the gate. The lookouts gave the all-clear.

'Very well then,' Philippa said, shaking Pearl's hand. 'Thank you for your hospitality. I will expect your decision by tomorrow.'

'Yes,' said Pearl. 'We will be in touch. One last thing – I'd like you to keep this.' She held out the pink soap. 'We have no use for only one bar.'

The debate on the integration of the beast-people into the life of the school was held in the assembly hall on the morning of the 27th of March 1977, just under two years after the end of the world. The resolution was: 'This house believes that the school should drive the beast-people from the island, by force if necessary.'

Because of the special significance of the debate, the running-order was slightly changed: the resolution had but one proposer, Pearl Wyss, and one defender, Laura Huxley. To give everyone a chance to participate, the seconds were replaced by an extended question-and-answer session from the floor.

The form of the resolution went unchallenged. Laura's camp seemed to feel that, in its uncompromising harshness, the resolution would be easy to oppose; and Pearl's camp seemed to feel that, in its adamantine clarity, the resolution would be easy to defend.

The debate was well attended. On some previous occasions, girls, fatigued from erecting fortifications, had been content to give such debates a miss. Not so now. This was, in some senses, the last debate. Up till now, everyone who dwelt on Near had been a scholar. Henceforth, everyone who dwelt on Near might not be a scholar.

Of course Murray Mint had never been a scholar. Though he was a very intellectual animal.

I had never seen Laura so happy. 'Cock-a-hoop' would be a fair description. The four youngest beast-men were by no means unattractive. They were good beast-marriage material. And the more we discovered about them – university students, carpenters, teachers – the more eligible they appeared to be, and the less compelling Pearl's vision of the cosmos.

Perhaps the beast-man was not, after all, a very representative beast-man.

Laura, in the past couple of years, had grown tall and pretty. She was seventeen but looked twenty-one. She took care of her hair. Her figure had 'filled out'. She spoke as if she had a hot razorbill egg in her mouth. She radiated the natural authority of her class, in that her every utterance, even the most commonplace, sounded intelligent and commanding.

Pearl, by contrast, was hobgoblin-esque in stature and appeared to lack sexuality. Her pronunciation was blandly Received. Her speech, while cogent, contained little in the way of wit, and her voice was simultaneously high-pitched and drab. She took no care of her hair, which seemed to be going grey.

She stood up with the patient smile of a girl convinced that she can persuade a roomful of teenage girls to jettison the only reasonable chance they might ever have of reproducing.

'I want you to look forward ten years,' she said.

Settling of bodies in plastic chairs.

'In ten years, each of the seven men outside these walls will have four or five wives. You will be their wives.' She pointed at her audience. 'You. Men are not content with just one wife if more are available. Men are not women. We, their wives, will be occupied in bearing their children. We will bear them, and we will look after them. We will labour for them. There will be boy children, and there will be girl children. The boy children will be the most valued. In ten years this island will have doubled in population. In thirty years it will have quadrupled.

'Thirty years from now, the school will be full of adult men and adult women. Man-warriors and woman-mothers. Just like any city-state in Earth's history. This island will have become overpopulated. We'll have eaten all the birds, cut down all the trees. The young men will be itching to prove themselves. They won't be content with defence. The ambitions of men include attack. So we'll try to expand. Of course, by that time, thirty or forty years hence, we'll be old women. No one will be interested in what we've got to say. Our male descendants, our grandchildren, will strike out from this place. They'll encounter other tribes from the mainland. There will be wars. Skirmishes, really. But there will be raped women and dead children, just the same. And as they fight and murder, we'll live in fear that they might not be successful, and that their enemies' revenge will include our rapes and our deaths. And so history will take its course. Just like before. Near will be like any other place on earth.'

She paused, changing gear.

'What is the position of a woman in a man's world?'

Not a very good one, I hazarded. I looked out of the window. I could see the beast-man on his bed. With some surprise I saw that he was reading a book. Perhaps, like the tent, it had been a decree of the school council.

'It's a subordinate position,' continued Pearl. '*We* do as *they* say. We bear their valued boy-children and we feed them our milk and wipe their bottoms. The men leave the drudgery to us, and they squabble amongst themselves for power. We have no control over our lives and we can't control our own future, our own culture. In this world of man-warriors and woman-mothers – woman-slaves – there's no room for chamber orchestras and painting pictures. Not for us, anyway. There's no time. We've got too much housework and childcare to do.'

Pearl, as I say, spoke without notes. Whether she memorised her speeches or not, I couldn't say. I assume she always knew what was coming next.

'So I am for separatism,' she said. 'I am for deciding our own future, and not having it decided for us by those seven men,' – she pointed – 'who, as I speak, wait outside to know whether we will allow them into these walls, to breed with us and to dominate us and our daughters. And not just for now. Forever.'

She sat down. Scattered applause.

Laura stood up, holding a sheaf of notes.

'Well, what a lot of nonsense,' she said, laughing. She waved her notes. 'I mean, what a lot of… rubbish. She makes them sound like savages. Men aren't savages. Not any more than we are. Do you really think those men out there are beast-men? You heard Philippa. They're Quakers. That means they're Christians.'

Noises of understanding.

'Christians. They want to live in peace. They've had enough of war. They're educated people. They could help us. They could improve our lives. We could have some of the things we don't have now. Like… like machines and practical things that men are good at. They can make things and build things. One of them's a carpenter, and one of them's a farmer.'

Laura looked out over her audience. She was dressed for the occasion, wearing a white shirt with a long pointed collar and a knee-length black skirt with high heels. She looked like a teacher.

'Who wants to live in a world with just girls in it? I'm not afraid to say it. Who wants to live without falling in love? Or getting married? Men are supposed to live with women. Men and women are two halves of the same coin. It says that in the Bible that Pearl is so fond of. Men and women have children together and they bring them up in families, and they try to make a better life for themselves. The man respects the woman and the woman respects the man. Each one has a job to do. I don't want to live for the rest of my life without knowing what that's like. And I *won't!* Pearl wants us to look forward ten years, twenty years, thirty years, a hundred years. But what does she really know about what will happen? Even next week? Is she some kind of wizard? This is an uncertain world. Things change quickly and things happen unexpectedly. We need every advantage we can get.

'I want you to look at what Pearl is really saying. She's saying we're so weak that we'll let those beastly men walk all over us. We're so stupid that we'll just be their slaves. Is that what Mrs Ballantyne taught us? We seem to have replaced Mrs Ballantyne with a new headmistress called Pearl Wyss. Mrs Ballantyne believed that girls can do anything. You can be whatever you want to be. You can make your way in the world as teachers or doctors or lawyers if you want. But Pearl says, no, you can't do anything, you're weak, you can't take control of your life.

'This isn't the Middle Ages. In the past, things were bad for women, but we've learned to do things differently. Go and look in the library. Go and see what women have achieved. It happened. In the old days no one knew better, and perhaps women *were* slaves. But we're not now. We won't forget. We are powerful, we have the knowledge. The library isn't going to disappear. Go and read about it. We don't have to have any more children than we want to. We can control how many we have.'

She consulted her notes.

'I want you to look at this argument that Pearl has proposed, that men are beasts and women are stupid. Look at it for what it is and ask yourself who it benefits. Let me tell you. It benefits Pearl. Her. So she can make *you* do what *she* wants. Why else do you think she keeps that man out there in that cage? He's useful to her. Who really loses if we go into a partnership with the... the newcomers? Pearl. Pearl is the one in control at the moment. Pearl, Pearl, Pearl. This is all really about Pearl, and her power. And she can't bear the idea of giving it up.

'Don't throw away this chance of a real life. Don't throw away the chance of having children. Without children this island's done for anyway. These men are our only real *hope* for a future. I don't say trust them immediately. Proceed with caution. But don't drive them away with violence. Do the sensible thing, not this mad thing that she wants you to do.'

She sat down to applause. Two rather interesting speeches, in fact. It is notable in life that one tends to be convinced by the person who speaks last.

Camilla Moon Khan in the chair opened up questions from the floor.

May Sussums put her hand on her head. 'I have a question for Pearl,' she said.

May Sussums, as well as a writer of *faux*-First-World-War poetry, was a rather unappetising girl with flaccid cheeks.

'Like Laura said,' said May, 'if we don't... you know, with the beast-men,' – she paused while those around her laughed – 'won't we just die out anyway? Then everyone will just be dead and there won't be any children to carry on after us anyway. So what will be the point of that?'

'I didn't say we shouldn't have children,' said Pearl. 'We can have children if we want.'

'How?' asked May Sussums.

Pearl, to my infinite surprise, pointed at me. 'Stephen.'

Collective intake of breath.

Horror.

Then – hilarity. Uproar. Peal upon peal of laughter.

'Stephen!' came the gleeful cry from all corners of the room. 'Stephen!'

Never before had I so eagerly wished for a lead-lined coffin to crawl into.

'Stephen! Stephen!'

A gaily-coloured balloon to whisk me upwards. Anything, to be away from these screaming banshees, my sisters, my harem.

Teenage girls are adept at prolonging hilarity. Finally it died away.

Laura seemed to feel she had found an opening. She turned her gaze to Pearl. 'All right,' she said, smiling. 'Let's say we do what you want. Let's say he gets us all pregnant.'

Squeals. Whether of delight or disgust, it was difficult to say.

'Then what happens?' Laura went on. She paused. 'What do we do with all the boys? The boy-babies?'

The hall quietened.

Brows were furrowed.

'Well,' said Pearl after a time. 'I suppose we have to hope there won't be any boys.'

Laura raised her eyebrows. 'You're being ridiculous,' she said. 'I'm asking you a serious question.' She leaned forward with ominous emphasis. 'What happens to all the boys?'

'And I'm telling you,' said Pearl, seemingly unperturbed, 'that we can't afford any boys. There won't be any. We'll just have to arrange it so there aren't any.'

Stunned silence.

'What do you mean?' asked Zillah, from the front row.

'Well, we'll have to control our population,' said Pearl. 'So we keep only the female babies.'

'You mean… kill the boys,' said Zillah.

'Yes,' said Pearl.

'Okay,' said Zillah, leaning back in her chair. 'That's what I thought you meant.'

'Are you joking?' exploded Laura. 'Because if that's a joke, it's not really the place for it. This is a serious debate.'

'No, I am not joking,' said Pearl. 'It's been practised in every culture in the world. In India, in China, in Japan, in Rome, even in England. Usually the mothers did it. In some parts of the world they still do – I mean, they did. And I suppose you know which babies had to go, don't you? Girls. Girls are second-best, after all. In every society on Earth, girls and women have always been second best. So they were weeded out. What I'm proposing is that we create the first society on Earth in which girls are first. We use Stephen to reproduce ourselves and we keep the girl children only. I'm sorry for the boy children but we can't afford them. We can't go back to a society in which women are second class citizens, and that's inevitable if men are around. It's been like that in every society on earth from the beginning of time. I don't want to live like that. Do you?'

The question hung in the air.

'I won't give up our future on the island,' Pearl said. 'So there is only one choice. Have children, but girls only. It is a girls' school, after all.'

Scratching of heads.

'So…' said Bee Wasket. 'How would we do it?'

'The Greeks exposed them to the elements,' said Pearl.

'Oh,' said Bee.

'Do you mean like plutonium?' asked Elizabeth Robinson.

'Elements, moron,' said Bee. 'The weather.'

'Weather?' said Elizabeth Robinson.

'Yeah,' said Bee. 'Rain. Wind.' She stuck out her lower lip, thinking. Then she shrugged. 'Well, I suppose that doesn't sound too bad.'

'Are you joking?' fulminated Laura. 'That's barbarian behaviour!'

'Don't call me a barbarian. You're the barbarian!' said Bee.

'Order!' said Camilla.

'I know it's horrible,' said Pearl. 'I'm not pretending it's not. But women have to do difficult things. Giving birth is difficult. Losing a baby for any reason is difficult. But when these things have to be faced, women can face them. They have faced them in the past. We can face them too.'

'Nonsense!' shouted Laura.

'Any more questions from the floor?' said Camilla.

'I have a question,' said Kat Egg, who wanted to be a doctor. 'What about when Stephen gets too old to be able to supply the necessary sperm?'

Cries of revolted merriment.

'We find someone else,' said Pearl. 'We'd need a new donor anyway. It wouldn't be healthy otherwise. In each generation we'll find a new one. There's no shortage of boys wanting to mate with females.'

'True,' said Francesca Mond from the third row.

'It's females who are the discriminating ones,' said Pearl. 'We choose. They don't care. They don't have to look after the children.'

This was news to me. I believed myself to be very discriminating.

'How do we find a boy?' asked Duenna Gee.

'Go to the mainland,' said Pearl. 'When we're ready. But that will be twenty years from now. Twenty years from now we'll have taught ourselves to sail. We'll be stronger. We'll have boats.'

'What if he didn't want to come?' said someone.

'Then we'd find one who did.'

A boy. A kidnap. Rather like a Viking raid. Only in reverse.

'Stupid,' said Laura.

'I have a question for Laura,' Alana March said. 'What about Pearl's point that the beast-men will want four of five wives each? How will you stop them?'

Laura looked both puzzled and annoyed. 'Does your pa have five wives? I don't understand. Do you know *anyone* who has five wives?'

'No,' said Alana, a little defensively.

'It's against the law,' said Laura. 'It's called poly something. We'll make it a law here as well. We'll make everyone agree. If anyone tries to do that, they'll be punished. It's not difficult.'

'What if,' said Francesca Mond, 'they just pretend to agree? Then afterwards we won't be able to stop them.'

'That's why I said proceed with caution,' said Laura. 'We don't let them in straight away. We get to know them, what kind of people they are, whether we can trust them. Then maybe when we know more, we have another debate. We don't just kill them all now.'

There were noises of agreement. I felt that this was Laura's best point yet. Nothing pleases like procrastination. In the contest between massacring-out-of-hand and waiting-and-seeing, waiting-and-seeing had considerable appeal.

Camilla Moon Khan in the chair turned to Pearl. 'What do you say to that?' she asked.

'I don't propose any immediate action,' Pearl said after a moment. 'I propose giving them time to think. Seven days. If they don't leave after that time, we take action. You see, there isn't much argument about what will happen if we "get to know them".'

Titters.

'I'm perfectly prepared,' Pearl continued, 'to admit they might be reasonable people. On the surface. Yes, they *are* just like your pa or your brothers. But underneath they are men, with men's nature. That doesn't change. The male nature can't be compromised with or appealed to. It's fixed. If they start off perfectly reasonably, that is because they're playing a game. They stand to win everything, after all. Think of it that way. We are the basis of their future power. We are the mothers of their children. Now look at it from the other side. What do we have to gain from them? Nothing. Nothing to gain, and everything to lose. We can find our own sperm any time we want to. We don't need them. Without them, *we* are in control. With them, *they* are in control. It's really as simple as that. As soon as we "get to know them", we take a step down the road to our own enslavement.'

'Laura?' asked Camilla chairpersonally.

Laura by this time was looking a little drained, but she rose to the challenge. She was still, after all, about two feet taller than Pearl.

'Enslavement,' she said bitterly. 'Let me tell you what Pearl's argument depends on. It all depends on… making men into devils.'

I found myself admiring Laura. In fact, she was beautiful. Or was it just her vowels?

'What Pearl never says is that men are people, and that women are people. If there were no men, why is she so confident that there would be no wars? I've read about this. I didn't write it down but I've got it here.' She reached beneath her chair and pulled a book from her handbag. I realised it was one of my mother's handbags. She riffled through the book. She found the place. 'The Spartan women said, "Come home with this shield or upon it".' She put the book down. 'That means come home victorious or come home dead. Women can be just as violent as men. What we have to do is create a society where no one is violent. That's where rules come in. And lawful punishments if people break the rules. Pearl likes to control everything. All punishments are through Pearl.'

'Isn't that *ad hominem*?' asked Robyn Loss-Stevenson from the front row.

'I don't care,' said Laura. 'I don't even know what that is. I'm talking about Pearl. The thing we're debating about is about a particular person and what she is capable of, and she's sitting over there.'

Pearl, sitting over there, bridled slightly, but said nothing. Robyn did have a point, I felt.

'Any more questions?' asked Camilla Moon Khan.

'Question for Pearl,' said a voice from the back. It was Titty.

'Yes, Titty.'

'Not all of us want to get pregnant by the method she mentioned.'

Laughter. I think it was at this moment that I began to hate Titania Pickering.

'No one has to do anything they don't want to,' said Pearl. 'If you're talking about sex, you don't have to have sex to get pregnant. You can do it artificially.'

'Like a cow?' said someone.

Kat Egg put her hand on her head. 'Sperm is a very powerful substance,' she said. 'Just some on your finger, if you put it inside yourself, you can get pregnant.'

Groans of distaste. Giggles of the opposite.

'Yes, that is correct,' Pearl said. 'A fertile woman can get pregnant very easily. There's no need to actually have sex.'

Sussurations. Comprehension. Pearl's plan now more palatable. Thanks to Titty. Titty having achieved the opposite of her intention.

'Any more questions?' asked Camilla Moon Khan. There was a pause. 'All right. I turn it over to the two principal speakers for summary rebuttal. Each speaker has three minutes. Laura won the toss to go last in the opening speeches, so she gets to go first in the summary rebuttals. Please stay within the time limit. I will tap a glass like this when you have ten seconds left.'

She held up a glass. She tapped it.

Laura stood up. She looked a little white. She licked her lips.

'I don't think this needs three minutes,' she said. 'But I'm going to take them anyway, because I know *she* will.' She put out one foot, pausing. 'You've all got to think very, very carefully about this decision. Please remember what the resolution says: "we drive them from the island by force if necessary". If Pearl wins, you're going to be fighting your first war. How ironic that would be. Wouldn't it?

'All right. Let's sum up what Pearl is saying. Pearl wants to *kill*' – with emphasis – 'these perfectly nice men, or drive them from the island, whichever is easiest. She then wants us to *mate* with perfectly nice Stephen' – laughter – 'and then have babies. Then she wants us to *kill* our babies. Our own babies. You'd have to be insane to vote for that. Baby-killing and man-killing. She must be out of her mind.

'Pearl can't see the future. She doesn't know what's going to happen in ten years. She's not interested in proceeding with caution, like I am. She wants them to be got rid of, now. Why? Because of her. Because of her power. Actually,' – Laura paused as if in thought – 'Pearl is the exact opposite of what she tells you she is. She's not for women and girls really. Because she actually thinks we're stupid and weak. Stupid women voting to be dominated by cavemen and beasts. If we voted for her we'd certainly be stupid. Neither is she really as peaceful and defensive as she says she is. She wants us to do what she said her sons and grandsons would do. Go out and kill whoever is in our way. Well, I for one won't be doing that, and I don't care if I win this debate or not.' Laura looked directly at her adversary. 'Times have changed, Pearl. We can organise society and do it better this time. I encourage you all, I beg you all, to oppose the resolution.'

Cheers. Clapping. Laura sitting down. I found myself clapping. I hadn't realised I was doing it.

Actually Laura hadn't taken anything like three minutes. The clock at the back of the stage said one minute and three quarters.

Pearl stood up.

'Let me deal with Laura's points,' she said. 'Firstly, if we drive the men off Near, it won't be a war. It will be self-defence. We'll give them seven whole days and we'll explain ourselves. If they choose to ignore us, they'll face the consequences. Because I'm not having any of those men telling us what to do. *Ever.*'

Pearl looked fierce as she pronounced this last word.

'Secondly, you don't have to mate with nice Stephen. Nice Stephen will help us out, that's all. Those who wish to have babies can have babies.

'Thirdly, girl babies only. All right, it's unpleasant. But let me remind you what just happened. There was a *nuclear war.*'

Again, anger. I had never seen Pearl so angry.

'There was a nuclear war that destroyed every city in Europe, and probably in America and Russia and God knows where else. Babies were killed, not by the twos or threes, but by the millions. By the hundreds of millions. Burned to death, or crushed, or by radiation. Why? Because of men! Their love of war. And I'm not going to see the same thing happening again.

'Fourthly, Laura says it's all about me. It's not about me. I want the school to carry on and survive and thrive. I want us to defend ourselves and control our futures. If someone else wants to take my place, run in an election against me! Defeat me in a debate! This is not a dictatorship. This is a democracy. But if you let those seven men in, soon you *will* be living in a dictatorship. The dictators will be men, and you will have to do what they tell you. Not because you are stupid and weak, but because of *what men are*. Men want power like… potatoes want water. They want to dominate. They fight among themselves for domination, and they go on and on until women are just exhausted trying to keep up with them.'

'Rubbish!' said Laura.

'Out of order!' said Camilla Moon Khan.

Pearl rounded on Laura. 'I want to *speak*!' she cried passionately. 'You spent the whole of your time telling me I was the problem, but I didn't interrupt *you*, did I?'

We gazed agog.

Pearl took a deep breath. 'Fifthly, I repeat, I want sensible defences and reasonable demands to those who wish to invade us and take us over. I want them to *go*. I don't want to control their lives. I don't care what they do with their lives. I want them to *get – off – our – property*! And sixthly, Laura, times have certainly changed. I couldn't agree more. Times have changed, but the nature of men hasn't.

'I offer you a vision. A city of girls and women. Secure on an island defended from all attack. Because we will extend our defences as our population expands. We will build walls to encompass the whole island. And they will not be of wood, but of stone. The new wall will take not a year, but a generation, each woman doing the work when she can. And our population. We will control it. The opportunity for everyone to have children if they want; those who don't, don't have to. Controlled so that the island can support us. Sufficient food for everyone's needs. One boy to be a father to all in each generation. No men here. No participation in any of the wars of the mainland. They are already fighting and killing each other over there! You heard this from two people: Edward and Philippa. Both of them told us – the fighting has started already! I want a life – for all of us – a life not of fear and drudgery and childbearing, while men hunt and despoil and fight, but a life of choice. To be poets or artists or scientists. Or musicians or engineers. Or to leave here if we wish. Yes, I offer anyone who disagrees this choice: go, if you wish. But if I win this debate, we will drive these men from this island. And anyone who joins them, we will drive them out too.'

Camilla Moon Khan tapped her glass.

Pearl fixed her gaze onto her audience. 'Okay, it's time for a vote. I want you to think about the future. But I also want you to think about the past. Think about the war. Think about what just happened. Think about who caused it and what we will have to do to stop another one. I beg you to support the resolution.'

Screams. Pounding of bow-stocks. War-whoops. Yells. Clapping. I found myself clapping again. I'd had no idea I was doing it.

'Let's vote,' said Camilla Moon Khan. 'Hands up, those for the resolution – that we should drive the beast-men from the island, by force if necessary.'

Little spinneys of hands. Girls nudging each other. Hesitant hands. More and more. Camilla Moon Khan's fingers pricking the air as she counted.

'Twenty-eight!' she cried.

Twenty-eight!

A majority!

Girls screaming. Getting up from their seats and embracing each other. Kisses. Passionate in some cases. I felt my body shudder. I buried my head in my hands. My shoulders shook. Edward Vane-Hovell-Vane. Stephen, Stephen. What have you done? What will you be required to do?

Camilla fought to be heard above the din. 'And against?'

But Laura was standing on the stage yelling. 'I can't believe it! She's got you! She's bewitched you!'

Pearl stood up, looking like a battered shampoo bottle.

'You're out of order!' screamed Camilla at Laura.

'I don't care!' Laura screamed back. 'Look at her! She's a witch! She's a witch!'

And indeed Pearl did look a little like a witch. Or perhaps something not entirely of this Earth.

'Those against!' screamed Camilla Moon Khan.

But everyone was ignoring her. Only a few, stony-faced, raised their hands.

'Five!' shouted Camilla Moon Khan. 'Five!' But the vote had been won. No one cared.

Pearl stood on the stage, unblinking.

Then she turned and walked down the little wooden steps.

And so Laura Huxley had once again been defeated. That makes this narrative very repetitive, I'm afraid. But if people behave according to type, patterns do tend to emerge. That is real life.

Notice was subsequently sent out to the band of beast-folk, the letter being inscribed by that talented calligrapher, Samara Slavens. It read as follows:

Please be informed of the Council's decision in re: your request of the 27th inst. to stay on Near. We regret that we cannot permit you to reside on the island. You have one week to comply with this decision. In one week, on or before the 3rd prox., you must leave, permanently. If you do not leave, or if you later attempt to land on Near, you will be met with lethal force. No further warning will be given.

With thanks for your past understanding, soliciting continuance of same,

Signed:

Pearl Wyss (Head of School, Captain of Darling), Mary-Dot Golding (Captain of Mancoe), Robyn Loss-Stevenson (Captain of Brownstone), Polly Findhorn (Captain of Wideopen), the above-signed representing the Council of the Near School for Girls, Near Island, Aberdeen, AB12 3LE

Copies of this decision are available on request.

The beast-party appeared to receive this missive with equanimity, but instead of leaving the island, took up residence at the Lodge.

The Lodge, by the spring of 1977, had been completely stripped of anything that a beast-man could desire. The roof had been removed by Bettina Farque. All furniture, beds, wardrobes, desks, etcetera, had been taken into the stockade, along with any books, documents, clothing, carpets, shelving, and so on. Pearl had moved into the Shute Building, one floor lower than, and a little toward the rear of, my own apartments, where she had a suite of rooms and an office.

The ground floor of the beast-Lodge, however, still had ceilings, and so was perfectly habitable. These were the seven or eight rooms that had once been Pearl's offices. And these the beast-people disappeared into.

They stayed there for three days. Then, on the morning of the 31st of March, they decamped. May Sussums saw them making their way back to the boat. Lookouts on the watchtower (Eunice Riddley and Lisa Plast) reported that they were setting up camp on the north-eastern shore. They seemed to be taking advantage of the local bird population. They showed no sign of wishing to depart.

Four days became five. The week was nearly up. Then, on the evening of the sixth day, Laura Huxley disappeared from the school.

She had let herself over the wall with a rope.

It was dusk on the seventh day.

The war-party had convened in the Shute Building. It consisted of the four house captains, Fritzi Merzig from Peitz (or Fritzi Peitz from Merzig), Tom and Henry Keck, Alana March, Zillah Smith, Karen Dworkin, and nine others, chiefly hunters and Pearlists. And myself. Twenty of us. Strong-armed girls, loose-limbed. Cropped heads. Painted, unwashed. Stockade-builders, well-diggers, ditch-diggers. Wood, water, earth.

'Your mission,' Pearl said to the party, 'is to eliminate the beast-men.'

'You mean kill them?' asked Robyn Loss-Stevenson.

'Yes,' said Pearl.

Zillah screamed and fainted. Someone dragged her to a corner and sat her up.

'We leave tomorrow morning before dawn,' said Pearl. 'We'll make our way to the north-east of the island and attack at first light. They'll be sleeping. If they're in shelters, we flush them out. Then we take them as they try to run.'

'What about Laura?' asked Tom Keck.

Pearl let out a long breath. 'Spare Laura,' she said.

'What about the woman?'

'If you can.'

'What?'

'Spare her.'

'So, kill all the men,' said Robyn Loss-Stevenson, pencil held aloft.

'Right,' said Pearl.

Scribbling. Silence and breathing. The scent of flowers and waxy hair.

'I know what you feel,' said Pearl. 'Women don't kill. We bring life. Not like men. But this isn't for the love of killing. This is protection, for the school, for our futures. We do this for our daughters. We do this for our grand-daughters. I don't hate these men. They're men. That's enough. They had their chance. I don't mean their seven days. I mean they had hundreds and thousands of years in which they fought wars, raped us, killed us and our children. And for no reason.'

There was a moan from the corner. Zillah.

Laughter.

'But we're not like them. We do this for a reason. We make war because we hate war. We won't stand for more war, centuries and centuries of war. We do it for this reason. Because we will not *be their slaves*!'

Thumping of bows. Ululations.

'They've been warned. Be ready at five. It's time to do what we must.'

By the time we got to the beach, the sky had lightened. It was chilly and still, and the waves were breaking murmurously. It had been difficult to get nineteen teenage girls out of bed at five o'clock in the morning.

We crept through the trees, our eyes on the grey gaps opening up in front of us. The beach. I gripped my bow, my mouth dry.

Pearl tiptoed ahead, light as a pine cone. She carried no bow. Close behind were her five trustiest lieutenants: Fritzi, Tom, Henry, Zillah and Bee. Behind them were the rest of us. We stopped at the fringe of the forest and peered out.

The men were already awake and seemed to be making tea on a campfire. A blackened kettle hung from a tripod. They sat cross-legged, meditative. Bones lay neatly in a waste-pit. None held weapons, but a bow lay propped against some bags a little way off. There was the familiar scent of roasted guillemot. Guillemot has a nutty aroma.

Philippa was nowhere to be seen, but Laura was there, sitting next to Cal. They weren't touching. Laura, it appeared, was in the opening phase of negotiations, or 'getting to know' the beast-men.

Cal spoke to the group. His words drifted in and out on the mild breeze. He was praying.

'Thank you for leading us safely to this place.... for your bounty on this island... help us gain the trust of those that live here... soften their hearts, O Lord... our desire to live in peace.... we join in saying the Lord's Prayer... Our father... lead us not into temptation... as we forgive them...'

I could see Laura's face. She seemed mystified.

Suddenly a scream rang out.

'It's them! It's them!'

It was Philippa, emerging from the forest a little way off. She ran for the boat, clumsily, holding her skirts up.

'Quickly!' she screamed. 'Get to the boat! To the boat!'

But this rather good advice was not heeded by any of the little group of deists. Cal simply stood up and stroked his beard. A younger man, who might have been Daniel, 'the baby', also stood up, frowning and stretching his arms.

From the tree-line, nineteen girls emerged at a jog-trot, bows drawn.

One of the older men, possibly Keith, made a stumbling run for the bow lying against the bags.

'Fire!' cried Pearl.

Two arrows sliced the air past him. The third hit him in his side. He doubled over with a grunt. Maud Colby lowered her bow and pushed hair out of her eyes.

'Fire!' screamed Pearl again.

A volley of arrows. The farmer, Michael, took a bolt to the neck. He began to stagger in circles, flapping at it. Richard was hit simultaneously in the leg, torso and head. An arrow protruded from his mouth and he fell down gushing blood. Daniel, Mark, Jacob and Cal ran for the boat, but Tom, Bee, Henry and Zillah pursued them and shot them at close range. Other girls, bringing up the rear, loosed further arrows into their bodies.

Now each man was down. Each had several arrows in him. Some lay still, others twisted horribly. I raised my bow and shot an arrow, missing everything but sand. I opened my eyes. There was Laura, right next to me. A little way off, I saw Robyn Loss-Stevenson raise her bow. I held my hands up.

'No!' screamed Laura at Robyn.

'No!' screamed Pearl.

Robyn drew her bow. At the same time, Laura ran between us. Robyn fired. The arrow struck Laura in the breast. She fell.

I threw myself to my knees in the wet sand. I put my hand on her warm wound. A single trickle of blood oozed from it.

'Laura!' I cried. 'Laura!'

I felt my own virginity and the waste of Laura's goodness. In that moment I loved her. I put my face near hers.

'I only wanted to get married,' she whispered.

Then her eyes were still.

We buried the men in separate graves by the tree-line. We removed the arrows first. They could be re-used.

It is not difficult to bury bodies in sand. Even large male bodies. Much may be dragged, if many girls are there to do the dragging. I think the story of the island rather goes to show that principle in action.

Some of the men's faces, in death, were oddly sagacious, as if they knew something we didn't. Others were bloody and gaping. Keith's face was the ugliest. He had taken longest.

I had vomited up last night's dinner.

Laura's body was carried back to the school to be interred by the graves of my mother, Yolanda Vane-Hovell-Vane, Edward Vane-Hovell-Vane and Barbara Pulmow.

Philippa, weeping and shuddering, was gently led to the school by Zillah Smith. I heard Zillah saying to her: 'Don't worry.'

It was a paradoxical morning. I certainly needed no further evidence of Laura's assertion that women could be as violent as men. I had nearly been killed myself. In the heat of battle Robyn had taken rather literally Pearl's injunction to 'kill all the men'. And yet this massacre had been in opposition to Laura.

After the burials, the girls turned their attention to the boat, bringing out its contents and dumping them on the beach. Clothing and boots for men. Hoods and capes. Apples in sacks, powerfully sweet. There must have been an orchard on Holy Island. Strange things: unknown medicines, a roasting-jack, some bottles of home-made wine, seeds, hammocks, matches, a further roll of sailcloth, some fruit-trees with their roots wrapped in canvas. Fishing nets, iron and copper wire. And finally, a coffee machine, with the coffee to go in it.

The boat, too. Our collection of boats now stood at three: the beast-man's rowboat, Edward Vane-Hovell-Vane's sailboat, and the beast-pilgrims' tugboat.

This story is coming to an end.

To recap: Pearl had won the debate. The beast-pilgrims had been slaughtered. Pearl's power had been consolidated. We were secure and free. Anything was possible. Poetry and novels might start being written, and so on.

Yet, after a fortnight, one of the more – shall we say – ticklish aspects of Pearl's programme had received no further mention.

On the morning of the 11th April, Pearl called me into her office.

Pearl stood with her back to me, looking out of the window. Either side of her, books were ranged from floor to ceiling. On the walls were photographs of Tabitha Shute, Nancy Astor and Margaret Thatcher, the first woman to lead a British political party. A bronze bust of Tabitha Shute stood in an alcove. Papers and files were piled on a substantial polished-wood desk. Pearl was an even more voracious reader than I was.

'Coffee?' she asked, without turning around.

'Yes, please,' I said.

'One cup of coffee for Stephen,' she called out. 'Well. What do you think of my idea for building a wall around the island?'

'I really don't know,' I said. 'It seems very ambitious.'

'Yes.' She turned away from the window. 'It's probably impossible. At the moment, anyway. What I mean is, at our current level of population. We'd need a lot more workers to do something like that.'

'More workers.'

'Yes.'

A pregnant pause. From the next room I could hear Henry tinkering with the coffee-maker, lighting the wood-burning stove.

'Yes,' she repeated. 'That's what I'm hoping you'll help us with.'

'Yes. Well...'

'I think you know what I'm saying. It's an opportunity.'

'I'm not sure I'm ready,' I said.

'You don't have to be ready. You're a man.'

'Won't the children want presents on their birthdays?'

Pearl smiled. 'I've always respected your intelligence, Stephen. That's why I'm going to be honest with you.'

'All right.'

'We're willing to give you this opportunity. But we can't allow you to remain on the island afterwards.'

'What?' I asked, astonished. 'Why not? I live here!'

'You are dangerous, Stephen. You are a nice man. That is not a very good example.'

'So Laura was right.'

'Of course she was. Quite a lot of what Laura said was right. But that's not the point of a debate. The point of a debate is to win.'

I heard my mother's voice. Show her what you're made of, Stephen! But when I thought of my mother I thought of Pearl. They seemed, now, to be the same person.

'You won't need to go straight away,' Pearl continued. 'Next year. March. Before you're eighteen. We'll do everything we can to help you, of course. I'm not unreasonable. We'll give you a boat, and supplies, and so on. You can take the sailboat or the rowboat. It's up to you. You can take one girl with you. I think I know which one.'

'You want to get rid of me because I'm too nice.'

'Yes.'

The smell of coffee began drifting into the room. It made me feel sick.

'Suppose I refuse.'

Pearl frowned. 'You wouldn't do that.' She walked to the window again. 'Why do you think, Stephen, that in traditional societies there is rejoicing when a son is born, and gloom when a daughter is born? Why are some girl-children murdered at birth?'

'I've no idea.'

'Because those traditional societies are wise,' said Pearl.

'What?'

'They are wise. A woman can only have a limited number of children. A dozen or so at the most. A man can have hundreds. If he is very determined. Or very lucky. Like you.' She smiled. 'A son – a son can spread his parents' genes far and wide. A daughter can only be prolific through her own sons. And who knows if she'll have any? A boy can start being prolific straight away.'

'I… what are you saying? That it's okay to murder girls?'

'Of course, a boy might not start to be prolific straight away,' Pearl said, ignoring me. 'He might be outcompeted by other men, who are more aggressive and therefore more attractive to women.'

'Just a moment,' I said, raising a finger. 'Just now… you said women find aggressive men attractive. That's what you just said.'

'Of course. Aggressive men defend their patrimony. They ward other men off. If they stay around, they might even bring in a bit of food. But that's not the main thing. The main thing is that they produce aggressive sons. And we like that. We women. We're not looking for any man to stick around, particularly. We can raise children on our own, with help from our mothers, our sisters, our aunts. What we're really looking for is a man who will get us pregnant and then abandon us. After he has sired a boy-child, of course. One that will turn out just like him.'

I couldn't quite believe what I was hearing. 'That sounds like the type of man you are actively trying to keep on the other side of that wall,' I said.

'Yes. It is.'

'So the island is based on a lie?'

'Certainly. Women will always want men. In the end, it will be impossible to keep them apart.'

'Why are you trying, then? Why not accept the inevitable?'

Pearl took a book from the wall. I saw a word on the cover: *Comfort*. She opened it, looked at a picture that I couldn't quite see, and snapped it shut. 'Because I don't want to get raped, Stephen. If you were a woman you'd know what I mean. I don't want to get invaded. What you forget is the power of culture. I can know I'm fated to lose, but at the same time want to put it off as long as possible. And so I deploy untruths – such as that women can live without men. But women can't live without men. This is the truth, no matter how high we build that wall.'

'Why are you telling me all this?'

'Because I owe it to you. I'm asking you to leave your home, after all.' A gimlet-eyed stare. 'Of course, I'm telling you all this in confidence. I would regard any breach of that confidence very seriously.'

'So – let me get this clear – you're going to turf me out, after I've done what you want. Why should I go along with it?'

'Why should you go along with it?' Pearl repeated. She appeared to ponder the question. Then she walked over to the communicating door. It was a heavy door, and doubtless well-soundproofed. She threw it open.

'Hello, Stephen!' came a chorus of voices.

In the other room were Maud Colby, Lettice Fine, Francesca Mond, Zillah Smith, Helen Maitland, Alana March, Julia Fitt-Matt, Beulah Gaze, Fritzi Merzig from Peitz (or Fritzi Peitz from Merzig), Samara Slavens, Eunice Riddley, Mary-Dot Golding, Alexandra Featherstonehaugh, Duenna Gee, Camilla Moon Khan, Anne Heaviside, May Sussums, Kat Egg, Elizabeth Pelham, Rowena Northcote-Heathcote, Harriet Gupping, Bee Wasket, Alice Celia Swash, Patsy Hugenoth and Eufemia Paleocapa.

'These are the ones who have elected to have sex with you individually,' said Pearl. 'There are twenty-six of us.'

'Us?'

'There are thirteen others who have elected to receive a sample, which you will provide at your convenience.'

The girls filed into the office and stood around laughing.

'Don't worry, Stephen,' said Zillah Smith. 'We won't hurt you.'

'It's going to be quite a lot of work,' said Pearl. 'But we'll have a timetable. Two a day. We'll wait until you've got as many pregnant as possible, and then we'll do it again after the first babies arrive – that is, for those who are unsuccessful.'

'You like girls, don't you Stephen?' asked Eufemia Paleocapa.

'I...'

'Of course,' said Pearl, 'I may have got it all completely wrong.'

'I...'

'But I don't think I have.'

Laughter. Girls crowding round me. Faces, lips, jewellery.

'I've tried him already,' said Bee Wasket.

'You haven't!' said Camilla Moon Khan.

'I…'

Pearl clapped her hands. 'All right,' she said. 'Stephen is a bit surprised, that's all. It's understandable. You've said hello, you can go. Please refer to the house noticeboards.'

Henry opened the double doors. The girls withdrew, talking loudly. I caught Fritzi gazing solemnly at me. I remembered what she had said – 'You're very serious, aren't you?'

'Have fun,' Mary-Dot Golding called over her shoulder.

The door closed behind them.

'As far as I am concerned,' Pearl said, 'I suppose we can start right away. Oh, and before that, I have something for you. Henry!'

The door to the reception room opened and Henry came in. She was bearing, in one hand, a cup of coffee, and in the other, a small brown bird.

'Albert!' I cried.

'Yes.'

'You took him?'

'Yes.'

'Why?'

Pearl considered. 'Well,' she said finally, 'I thought I would use him to persuade you to help us. But I never needed him.'

'That was unnecessary,' I said. 'I missed him.'

'I know. But you won't be lonely now.'

Albert flew from Henry's hand and perched on my shoulder. It was like old times. I suddenly felt a surge of happiness. There wasn't much point opposing Pearl. You were liable to get yourself shot.

'You know,' I said, stroking Albert's breast with my finger, 'it strikes me that you could have saved yourself a lot of trouble and just used the beast-man in the first place.'

'Yes, that has occurred to me,' said Pearl. 'But, you see, back then, we were weak. We were powerless. We had no way to keep others out. Perhaps he would have called his friends to share in his good fortune.'

'Yes. I suppose.'

'Laura was right, in her way.' Pearl undid the top button of her school blouse. 'It is, finally, about power.'

I will leave to the reader's imagination the events of the following eleven months. I assume the reader is old enough.

But hold hard, I hear you cry. It's just getting interesting. How did you achieve it, exactly? Did you really have sex twice a day, every day? What exactly were the… arrangements? What…?

But sexual intercourse, while a consuming interest of all people of all climes, is, if both parties are willing, inherently undramatic. The effect is curiously like marriage, where romance conventionally ends. 'And they lived happily ever after.' There is nothing of very great moment in being a sperm fountain. Liberated from the diktats and prohibitions of both mother and father, and with a harem of girls monotonously offering themselves to his person, our hero presents a dolefully dull picture, a satrap surrounded by his odalisques.

I was, I supposed, in the position the beast-man had envisaged for himself.

I was expelled on the 25th March 1978, not long before my eighteenth birthday. By then I had sired seventeen girl-children, whether directly or indirectly. A further twenty pregnancies awaited their outcomes.

Pearl gave birth to a boy. He shared the fate of all boys.

I took no female companion. I did ask. Sam Keller thanked me but said she had a baby now. Melissa Verne said she felt safer on the island. Fritzi Merzig from Peitz (or Fritzi Peitz from Merzig) said she didn't love me. Kat Egg wished to stay near the school dispensary. Camilla Moon Khan doubted my sincerity. Ludivine Nockolds failed to give a reply.

I didn't ask Titty.

I was given supplies for two years, chiefly in the form of powdered soup and dried seal. I took the rowboat. I lack the practical sense for sailing.

Here on the mainland I rely more on stealth than on fortification. The point of fortification is to defend something in plain view. Stealth has no need of fortification. I will not specify exactly where I live, nor how I have protected myself.

Albert flits hither and thither as I write this. He cheers me up. He is an old pipit now.

I have spent the last two years doing very little. I have grown a beard. My life consists of eating soup and writing, at the rate of about two litres and 500 words a day.

I suppose I do see things a little more clearly these days. Pearl was right to expel me. In fact, everything she did was right. In the months before I left, she reminded me more and more of a certain person. She even started doing the crossword puzzles in some of the old newspapers in the art room. Occasionally – though with less and less frequency – I was able to assist her with a clue.

If there was one thing she did wrong, it was to let me leave the island alive.

For over there, on Near, is everything a man could need. Food, water, shelter, culture – and women. A society ripe for conquest. One decapitating blow could destroy it. Remove Pearl, and you would remove the ideology that sustains the experiment. Unfortunate, of course. But Pearl herself told me she was fated to lose.

All I will need is some confederates. Beast-men, if you will. Cortes conquered Mexico with a handful of be-whiskered and foul-smelling Spaniards. A new Cortes for Near would need three things: men, weapons and an understanding of the mind of his adversary.

And then, Titty, you will be mine. Whether you want it or no.

The beast-man will be freed. It's the least I can do.

Yes. Confederates. I must seek them out. Though, so far, my neighbours here have not proved congenial.

I have never been very good at making friends with boys.

About the Author

Gary Dexter has published three novels, *The Oxford Despoiler* (2009), *All the Materials for a Midnight Feast* (2012) and *Natural Desire in Healthy Women* (2014), as well as numerous non-fiction books. Now and then he writes short auto-biographies such as this one. He currently lives in Tokyo.

ALSO FROM NEWCON PRESS

Best of British Science Fiction 2023 – Donna Scott
The annual showcase of British SF, now in its eighth year. The very best science fiction stories by British and British-based authors published during 2023. A thrilling blend of the cutting-edge and the traditional from Alastair Reynolds, Jaine Fenn, Stephen Baxter, Adrian Tchaikovsky, Lavie Tidhar, Ana Sun, Chris Beckett, Ian Watson, Fiona Moore, Tim Major, & more.

A Jura for Julia – Ken MacLeod
The first collection in eighteen years from multiple award-winning science fiction author Ken MacLeod. His finest previously published short stories and novelettes from that period along with a new story written specially for this collection. The volume benefits from cover art and internal illustrations by award-winning artist **Fangorn**.

Dark Shepherd – Fred Gambino
Breel is abruptly fired from her dead-end job at the Beach, dismantling junked spaceships – a job she only took to help support her ailing father. She's convinced things can't get any worse; until people start shooting at her. A thrilling space opera that will leave readers wanting more.

Back Through the Flaming Door – Liz Williams
A new Fallow Sisters story; a new Inspector Chen story set in Singapore Three; a new tale set on the Matriarchal Mars of *Winterstrike*; a new story from the world of *Bloodmind*… All this and more in Liz Williams' stunning new collection. Thirty-two stories that enchant, dazzle, and blur genre boundaries. Take a deep breath and leap in.

To the Stars and Back – edited by Ian Whates
All new short stories and novelettes written in honour of the much-missed **Eric Brown**: (May 1960 – March 2023) by his fellow writers and friends, including Alastair Reynolds, Justina Robson, Chris Beckett, Una McCormack, Ian Watson, Tony Ballantyne, Keith Brooke, Philip Palmer, James Lovegrove, Kim Lakin, and more

www.newconpress.co.uk

Milton Keynes UK
Ingram Content Group UK Ltd.
UKHW010111130624
443943UK00004B/62

9 781914 953859